PAYBACK
IN SPADES

BY

D. W. DRAKE

COPYRIGHT

TABLE OF CONTENTS

CHAPTER ONE

FAIRFAX DISTRICT
LOS ANGELES
NOVEMBER 14, 1951
8:40 A.M.

The scalding jets of water had turned the skin on my naked body a pleasing shade of pink except for the ugly, indented, plum-sized scar on the outside of my left leg which was by contrast an angry, protesting red. I liked my showers just a little hotter than I could stand, maybe because it felt so good when I turned the water off. The ugly scar on my left leg was the healed result of a wound from a Japanese hand grenade that exploded near me while I was serving with the Marines on the island of Guadalcanal a war-and-a-half ago. The wound had left me a semi-cripple and compelled me to change my civilian occupation from police detective to private investigator.

The same grenade that had mangled my leg had also fractured my skull. The explosion must have screwed up the electrical connections in my brain because since being wounded I have been plagued by voices constantly chattering away inside of my head. It's no wonder that people I interact with often think me a little crazy. Hell, I'm probably as crazy as one of those nuts who sit naked out in the desert and bay at the moon, but the constant conversations going on inside my head that only I can hear are extremely grating on me, proving that even crazy people can get annoyed.

The first voice I call "Captain Straight." He speaks for the reasonable, mostly sane, analytical part of my brain. Most of the time he sounds like a harried kindergarten teacher trying to keep me out of trouble instigated by another voice constantly gabbing away in there that I call, "The Brat." He represents the secret selfish part of my being that everyone has but keeps private and never shows to the world. He is also a smartass and is responsible for most of the off the wall things I say.

The third and final secret voice represents my libido. Most of the time he is content to stay down there south of my waist and remain dormant, but whenever any reasonably attractive female gets within range, he eagerly attempts to take over my brain, wanting to run things. Because he only cares about sex, he doesn't talk all that often and much less than the other two voices. Because of his close association with my male member, I refer to both this voice and my penis as "Little Matt."

As I was rinsing the last of the soap from my body, Captain Straight and The Brat were arguing about one of the naturally occurring patterns in a section of the marble shower wall in the bathroom adjoining the master bedroom of the bungalow I share with my wife and baby son.

The Brat: "It looks like Hairy Ass Truman sitting on the pot."

Captain Straight: "Nonsense, anyone can tell it looks more like a naked Lady Godiva with her long flowing hair riding her horse side saddle."

The Brat: "Bullshit, how do you get a naked babe out of that? You must have a screw loose if you don't see old Harry sitting there and looking all stern and presidential."

I was of necessity staring at the same little squiggle in the stone because my voices didn't have eyes of their own and had to look through mine to see anything. To me, the jumbled pattern in the marble only looked like the after effects of the bursting of a gas bubble that formed in the silt on the bottom of an ancient Italian lake back when Tallulah Bankhead was but a slip of a girl.

"Come on guys, do you have to argue about everything?" I asked out loud. "Can't you just shut the hell up for a while and let me enjoy my shower?"

The Brat: "There you go thinking only of yourself again. The captain and I don't have arms and legs. So we can't go outside for a stroll, drive to Yellowstone National Park or go down to the corner bar and lift a few on our own. All we can do is talk, and now you want to take that away from us."

I didn't reply but just sighed and shut the water off. I stepped from the shower and reached for a towel. Despite the voices I was feeling really good that morning. I had slept like a log and felt rested and ready for a day tracking down clues at the detective agency I owned. I glanced out the bathroom window. The weak November sun was shining in the east facing window and I could see the leaves on the pear tree in the backyard shimmering, meaning there was a nice breeze blowing. November in Los Angeles was different than in most American cities. When I walked out of my door later I could expect temperatures in the seventies.

As I toweled my body off I happened to glance at my reflection in the full length mirror screwed to the opposite wall. Like all men secretly do when they are naked, alone and staring at their image in a mirror, I sucked in my gut, threw out my chest and flexed my biceps. I didn't look so bad for thirty-eight. I was no Charles Atlas, but the muscle tone in my lanky, six-foot body was still pretty good save for the waist, which was noticeably thicker than when I was in my twenties. I didn't worry about that because the tailoring in the expensive, custom made suits I wore would hide that for some time to come. Little Matt looked the same as when I was twenty. I wondered what his secret was. My receding hair, however, was starting to worry me. I had been blessed with a head of ample, dark brown, wavy hair. It had been, along with my sort of handsome face, one of my best features. I still had plenty of hair but the problem was it was receding up my forehead at double the velocity of your average Alaska glacier. So far though, I didn't have a bald spot up on top and for that I was thankful.

"Okay, Tarzan, if you can take a break from preening for the mirror, I have a bone to pick with you."

I was so engrossed in my image in the mirror that I hadn't noticed that my wife had entered the bathroom carrying my baby son on her right hip, wearing only a diaper-my son, not my wife.

My lovely wife June was a former airline stewardess. She was tall, slim and elegant, yet curvy in the right places. A natural blonde, she had huge, wide-set, blue eyes, a perfect nose and full lips that just begged to be kissed. At least that was the way she looked when we got married two years ago. This morning she appeared a bit different. Her blonde hair looked like a couple of rats had had a fight to the death amid her shiny locks, her skin was pale, the whites of her big blue eyes were shot through with red veins and there were dark half-moon circles under them. She was wearing a rumpled housecoat with a baby vomit stain on the left lapel.

Resting on my wife's right hip was my son and heir, Robert Matthew Cole II, eight months old. We called him "Bobby," but of late I had taken to referring to him as "Winston" because of his uncanny resemblance to the wartime British leader, Winston Churchill. My son had the same pink skin, multiple chins, chubby cheeks and bald pate with three hairs carefully oiled and combed over. All that was missing to complete the picture was the long black cigar jutting from his mouth. But my boy Winston was too young to smoke cigars and wouldn't be able to light up his first panatela for quite a while yet, at least six months or so. At that moment Winston was looking at me with the same ill-tempered scowl he had last displayed when he had first been told that the entire British Expeditionary Force was bottled up by the Germans in Dunkirk, with their backs to the sea.

"Good morning, sugar," I said to my wife brightly.

"Don't sugar me. I'm not in the mood. I've got a colicky baby and I haven't slept for three nights. He started yelling at two a.m. and hasn't stopped since," said June.

"Why didn't you wake me up? I would have taken care of him."

"I tried. Why is it that when a floor joist creaks in this old house you jump up like a cat and prowl the house naked with a gun in your hand, but when I wake you up to go tend to the baby you say 'sure thing, sugar' and then immediately start snoring again?"

At this juncture Winston's facial expression changed for just an instant from one of stern disapproval to one of sympathy. It was if he was saying, "I'd like to help you but I have to go with the one with the containers full of delicious milk. They even have these nifty dispensers built right in. All you have to do is suck on them and you get all the milk you want. I'm sorry but you're on your own, pal."

"I have no recollection of being woken up. You should have been more forceful," I responded.

"You're right. I'll tell you what. I'll go get a claw hammer from the garage and keep it by the bed to wake you up with. I'll have to be careful how hard I hit you in the head with it though; I might kill you and get arrested. Answer a question mister big shot private eye, will they allow me to breast feed in jail and allow me to sleep late? If they will, it might be worth it."

One of Winston's eyebrows shot up and he gave me a new look as if to infer, "You're not representing the male sex very well so far in this argument. I'm disappointed in you."

I decided to grovel. It was the only way out I could see. "I'm so sorry for not helping you with the baby. Will you forgive me?" I pleaded while giving her the puppy eyes routine. June stopped talking and gave me a measured look, but I could tell she wasn't ready to let me off the hook just yet.

"How did I get myself in this predicament? A couple of years ago I was single, carefree, flying to interesting places, wearing pretty clothes and being flirted with by handsome men. Then you chased me down and talked me into marrying you and look at me now. I'm hooked up with a guy that has a peanut gallery full of oddball voices in his head that talk to him all the time and he's the biggest slob God ever created. Haven't you noticed that your underwear drawer is empty?" she asked.

"Well, as a matter of fact, I was going to ask you about that," I replied.

"Do you remember me asking you politely about a hundred times not to leave your dirty underwear on the bathroom floor every evening?"

"Yeah, I vaguely recall that."

"Do you also recall that I told you two weeks ago that if you continued leaving your soiled linen on the floor, I would assume that your dirty drawers were just pieces of trash that you wanted me to throw out."

"No, I don't remember you saying that. But I could ask Captain Straight. He remembers everything," I replied.

"Never mind, I did say it and I also have been throwing out your underwear one piece at a time for a couple of weeks," said June and then grimaced. "Would you hold your son for a moment, I can't feel my arm."

I reached out my arms to take Winston. But he was having none of it. His eyes grew wide and his face contorted into a rictus of terror. He threw his arms around my wife's neck in a death grip and held on for dear life. If Winston had been a little stronger he might have throttled her right there. June just looked exasperated and shifted the baby to her other side.

For the first six months of his life, Winston had been my buddy. He would gurgle, grin and poke spit soaked fingers in my eyes, mouth and ears when I held him. Then, all of a sudden he began acting like I was one of Josef Stalin's NKVD torturers about to work him over with a rubber hose.

It was obvious that my groveling wasn't working. Our little talk had reached the point where I had two choices. I could abjectly surrender and be a gelding for the rest of our marriage, or I could counterattack. I chose the latter.

"June, sweetie, you're exhausted. But it doesn't have to be this way. When my dad died he left me over two million dollars. We can well afford a nanny for the baby. In fact we could afford a platoon of nannies. Winston would get more attention than Rita Hayworth naked in Times Square. As for the housework, we could hire maids. We could even afford an upstairs maid even though we don't have an upstairs. She could just straddle the roof peak with binoculars and be on the lookout for incoming Russian bombers."

An expression of incredulity appeared on June's face. "Let me get this straight. You want to allow a stranger to raise our child and other strangers to clean my house for me when I am perfectly capable of doing it myself? I have never heard anything so ridiculous in my life. My mother would be scandalized."

"There you go. Just when we're having a nice, normal, married couple discussion, you have to go and ruin it by mentioning Helga, the Viking Queen," I said.

"I think it's time for you and my mother to end this little feud you have going. If each of you would just bend a little bit you might find that you could learn to like each other."

June's mother Helga was tall like her daughter but, unlike her daughter, she was built like a lineman for the Chicago Bears and had the surly disposition of a wolverine whose den had just been taken over by a passing badger. Helga grew up on a farm in North Dakota. In my mind's eye I could see her coming in from the fields after a hard day of poking the plow horse in the ass with a sharp stick to make him go faster, with an oaken bucket of well water balanced on her pinned up blonde pigtails and a full grown sheep tucked under each arm. She thought I drank too much, smoked too much and that her daughter was much too good for the likes of me. I thought she was the most opinionated, surly person I had ever run into. She had a maddening habit of quoting old, trite adages like "birds of a feather flock together" or "better safe than sorry," always prefaced with the phrase "As my uncle Ole often said." It was enough to turn the Pope into a homicidal maniac, lopping off the heads of the nearest altar boys with a crusader sword looted from one of the Vatican tombs. June's father Warren, however, liked me, probably because I was rich and because I slipped him five grand or so every six months for his latest crackpot business scheme.

"No, thanks," I replied. "I had a nightmare about Helga night before last. In my dream she broke down our bedroom door wearing a battered iron breastplate, with her blonde pigtails poking out from under a battle-scarred, conical, horned steel helmet and menacing me with a battle ax dripping with the blood of ninth century Irish monks. The Viking Queen chased me all over the house trying to chop off Little Matt while all the time yelling in a maniacal voice 'as my uncle Ole often said, a stitch in time saves nine!'"

"Very funny," retorted June. "You missed your calling. You should be on the Jack Benny Show. My mother is a sweet, generous and kind person who wouldn't hurt a fly."

"Okay, flies are safe, but her sons-in-law who are private detectives, plow horses with hemorrhoids and every other form of critter better watch out. As Uncle Ole often said, 'never trust a black hearted Swedish woman with the size and disposition of King Kong.'"

"Okay, that's enough of your comments about my mother!" said June with fire in her eyes.

The Brat: "What's wrong with this babe today? Do you think her hormones are out of whack?"

"The Brat says you may need to have your hormones checked," I said out loud.

"You tell The Brat that he better not say that again or that head he lives in rent free will be found severed from its body and bobbing around in Santa Monica Bay," said my wife hotly as she left the room with Winston peering imperially back at me over her shoulder. The Brat shut up after that. He didn't say a thing for a while. I don't think he was sure if June was serious or not.

As I finished dressing I mused to myself about the change in my wife since our wedding. In the beginning she was so sweet, kind and accommodating. Now she was almost as much of a wise ass as me. I wondered how this change had come about.

Captain Straight: "I think you will find the answer to your question by looking in that mirror over there."

CHAPTER TWO

When June and I returned from our honeymoon, we came back to my apartment to live temporarily until we could find a house to buy. When she walked in the door to my place for the first time, my new wife's mouth dropped open in shock and she dropped her suitcase on the floor. She then tied a rag around her hair and proceeded to fill up the trash cans in the alley with all my prized possessions. Gone was my prized empty beer bottle collection, my stack of Life magazines going back to 1938, my life sized plaster deer, my old police uniforms, fourteen pairs of worn out shoes, a nifty beaded curtain that I had used as a door to my bedroom, and a bunch of other valuable stuff that I can't remember right now. She then proceeded to scrub every surface in the room with soap and water with the rigor of an army chemical warfare decontamination squad.

This irrational behavior was my first hint that Helga, the Viking Queen had instilled all kinds of undesirable vices in my wife when she was growing up. Things like excessive cleanliness, neatness, thrift, sobriety, self-control, always telling the truth no matter what the cost and many other harmful traits that went against the grain of Los Angeles society at the midpoint of the twentieth century.

So it was no surprise that when I offered to buy her a mansion in Beverly Hills, she turned me down. "What do you think I am some pampered, entitled female swell with a nasty little white dog?" she asked. "I just want a normal house and nothing pretentious." We ended up buying a bungalow on a quiet street in the Fairfax District of Los Angeles, not far from the rooming house I had lived in when I came back from the war. This bungalow was a bit larger than its neighbors. It was just a tad over two thousand square feet with a big eat-in kitchen, three nice sized bedrooms and two bathrooms. The extra bathroom turned out to be a problem for, of all people, The Brat. "Why the hell do you need two bathrooms?" he remarked in his typical sarcastic tone. "You can only crap in one toilet at a time. Besides, if you offer houseguests a bedroom with a private bath, the bastards will never leave."

§

FAIRFAX DISTRICT
LOS ANGELES
NOVEMBER 14, 1951
8:35 A.M.

As I made my way out the kitchen door on my way to the detached garage, besides my usual limp, I was walking a little bow legged too. This was to keep the wool fabric of my suit trouser inseam from scratching my bare balls. I was also crammed to the gills with food. Apparently another of the practices that the Viking Queen instilled in my wife was to never let a man leave the house without him being stuffed like a turkey on Thanksgiving Day. This was a fine practice if the stuffee was a farm worker needing fuel for a hard day setting fence posts or plowing behind a horse. But to a guy like me, whose idea of strenuous activity was taking out the garbage cans once a week, it was just a wee bit excessive. This was the reason my waist size had expanded by three inches since I entered wedded bliss. I had just finished devouring enormous portions of eggs, ham, fried potatoes, buttered toast and waffles slathered with butter and maple syrup, all the while with Winston eying me warily across the table while sitting in his high chair and gumming the handle of a big wooden spoon. I wondered what was really going on behind those beady little eyes. Probably some nefarious scheme to get Stalin to invite the entire British Labour Party leadership to Moscow for a visit and then not let them leave but pack them off to Siberia instead.

I slid open the big door on my one-car garage and beheld my pride and joy. It was a new, Inverness Green, 1952 Cadillac, series, 62 Coupe de Ville, two door hardtop. It sported a hydromantic transmission, velvet toned radio, fender skirts that obscured the top half of the rear white side wall tires and two huge chrome bullets that jutted forward from the front bumper. When I first got the car I wondered what their function was. Then I figured it out. If I should happen to plow into a herd of pedestrians, the bullets would impale the unfortunate people before they could smash up my fancy grill. Those Cadillac engineers had thought of everything. I opened the driver's door, got in and started the motor, then backed out of my driveway and headed for A-1 Discrete Investigations, my detective agency located on Wilshire Boulevard.

I arrived at my office about an hour later and parked in one of the two slots reserved for me in the tiny parking lot at the front of the building. Parked in my other slot was a black, 1946 Ford sedan with oxidized paint, a few minor dents, dirty windows and missing left front hubcap. This was my work car. It wouldn't do for a detective to drive a fancy new car to some of the places I had to go on a daily basis. It would attract too much attention.

The reason it had taken me an hour to go the few miles from my home to work was that I made a stop along the way at a J.C. Penney store. I arrived there just as the place opened and purchased their entire stock of size 36 male underwear, including a stack of boxer shorts with little cupids printed on them. I had to drive around to the loading dock at the rear of the store so a sweating stock boy could load the cartons in the trunk of my Caddie. My lovely wife thought she had triumphed in the underwear war, but in reality she had only won the first battle. Thanks to my recent purchase I now had enough ammunition to prolong the conflict for another three months. We would see who cracked first. Being rich has its advantages. I could afford to do petty things like this whereas the usual working stiff would have to retaliate in a more modest way. But if the truth were told, besides the fancy suits and new car every year, I lived about the same as when I was poor. I had everything I wanted, but I didn't want too much.

My detective agency occupied one-half of the second floor of a modern six story building on Wilshire Boulevard. The building was as tall as you could build in Los Angeles. According to the law no structure could be taller than 150 feet. The décor of my office was all steel and glass and polished wood with framed prints of horses hung in strategic places throughout the waiting room. For the umpteenth time I wondered what the hell horses had to do with detective work but it didn't matter. My office manager, Miss Caroline Adderley, only looked at me like I was an idiot whenever I asked her about the pictures. As I limped in from the hall I saw four nervous young women and a few older men sitting on the hard sofas and chairs in the waiting room. It looked like business was good that day. Straight ahead of me, sitting at her station behind a polished wood counter, was the company receptionist, Betty. She was a mousy looking, nervous woman for whom the decade past thirty had not been kind. She had the headset for the PBX clamped to her head with the mouthpiece on a stiff wire alongside her jaw. When she saw me coming, she shot her body up straight from a slouch and gave me a nervous smile.

"Good morning, Mr. Cole. Mrs. Adderley has been looking all over for you. Just a moment, I'll buzz her line," she said, and fiddled with some switches or doodads out of my sight. A few seconds later Betty said into her mouthpiece "Mrs. Adderley, Mr. Cole just arrived. He's at the front counter." There was a pause and then she said "yes, Mrs. Adderley." Then to me, Betty said,

"Mrs. Adderley says for you to not move a muscle. She'll be right here." I got the distinct impression that I had done something terrible and a squad of pointy headed goons was about to storm into the room, swarm me and take me to the floor.

The Brat: "You didn't tell anyone that you hear voices in your head did you?"

Captain Straight: "Shut the hell up. The last thing we need is for Matt to answer you out loud and confirm he's crazy as that preacher in the news who is sitting up in the Hollywood Hills saying the world is gonna end next week."

I heard footsteps behind me and turned and saw my office manager, Mrs. Caroline Adderley, striding toward me followed by her assistant, LuAnn. Caroline was a tall woman in her sixties who wore her gray hair pulled back in a tight bun and perpetually displayed an expression of suppressed displeasure. As usual she was wearing a severe looking woman's business suit. Luann, her assistant, was a medium sized woman of about forty who was tenser than Robin Hood's bowstring. Terrorized on a regular basis by her boss, she normally hovered close to hysteria most of the time. But today I could tell she was having a good day. Only one eye was twitching.

Almost from the moment that I hired her, Caroline and I had been engaged in a war of wills to determine who would be the big cheese at my detective agency. Recently, becoming tired of the conflict, we had settled on a compromise. She would run the place and I would stay out of her way. I did manage, however, to wring a few teeny weeny concessions from her before the surrender.

Caroline's normal expression when looking at me was that of a hawk who had just spied a fat, juicy field mouse. Today's was different. She stared at me like I'm sure Sitting Bull looked at General Custer at the Battle of the Little Bighorn. It looked like "Yellow Hair" was about to get his comeuppance.

"Your office," Caroline said, as she stormed past me. I was forced to fall in line behind Luann and follow them like a third wife in the Han Dynasty. Once inside my spacious office with its modern, classy, expensive furnishings, Caroline turned the blowtorch of her angry gaze on me.

"Do you recall that I reminded you three times yesterday that we were to conduct interviews of prospective female detectives this morning and that you had to be here before nine?" she asked like Perry Mason moving in for the kill.

"Oh, yeah, I remember that now." I replied sheepishly.

"Really, Matthew Cole, it's almost eleven. When you do these inconsiderate things you make this agency and my management look very unprofessional. I was here at nine. The applicants were here at nine. The only missing component was you, which is strange considering the fact that you were the one who championed the idea of hiring a female detective in the first place. As you recall I was against it, but as you have the final say as to whom we hire and let go, I set up the interviews to try to fulfill your wishes."

I felt uncomfortable under Caroline's disapproving gaze so I shifted my eyes to Luann who was standing behind Caroline. The tension in the room must have really heightened because both of Luann's eyes were twitching now.

"I want you to sit here and not move a muscle while I go and escort the first applicant back here," said Caroline. "Don't go out in the hall for a smoke. Don't decide to walk down to the corner bar for a snort or wander into the bullpen to exchange windy, made up war stories with Bill Stout." Bill Stout was one of my detectives that had also served in the Marines during the Pacific War. We often swapped war stories but most of them were true, I swear. Well, at least some of them were true.

After Caroline left and I was alone, I asked out loud, "Why didn't one of you assholes remind me I had to be at the office at nine?"

The Brat: "Don't look at me. I'm not supposed to be the responsible one, the captain is."

Captain Straight: "Okay, I'll take the heat for it, but let's face it, you could have written a note to yourself or told your wife to wake you early or something."

While I waited I looked at my mail and messages which I found in a neat stack on top of my desk. Most of it was advertisements and mundane matters that I didn't care about so I chucked them over my shoulder in the general direction of the trash can. One envelope caught my attention, however. It was addressed to "Matthew Cole, personal and private." I opened the legal size Manilla envelope and shook out the contents on the desktop. The first thing that caught my eye in the small pile of items from the envelope was two crisp, new one hundred dollar bills folded in half, each displaying my favorite portrait of Benjamin Franklin. I'm sure you've seen it many times. Old Ben's tilted a little to the side from sitting on his fat wallet. The presence of the money piqued my interest and I examined the other pieces of paper in the pile.

The next item I picked up was a ticket to a professional wrestling match at the Olympic Auditorium. I looked closer and discovered that the ticket was for tonight's show. I say "show" and not "contest" because as everyone in L.A. knew, pro wrestling was far from being a sporting event. The matches were fake and choreographed tighter than a Busby Berkeley musical. That didn't stop pro wrestling from being wildly popular among the working classes in Los Angeles. KTLA, one of the three television stations in town, carried the matches and broadcasted them live every Wednesday night to those families who could afford to own television sets. Whole groups of people, including the neighbors of the owners of the sets, would sit glued to the flickering, grainy screens, not caring that it was ruining their eyesight. The last item in the pile was a folded handwritten note on lined notepaper. In legible cursive, the note read:

"I need you to do a job for me. Come see me tonight in dressing room G after the second bout." The note was signed with an enigmatic "C."

This was a poser for me. Who the hell was C? Off the top of my head the only people I knew whose names started with the letter C were Caroline Adderley, Carlo the mountain-and-a-half and a dancer named Cindy who I met and stopped seeing long before I married my wife and I hadn't seen since. Well, maybe last year I saw her in the chorus line at the Copa Club but that's all. I promise.

Captain Straight: "I'll back Matt up on that. I haven't seen him with that dancer in ages."

The Brat: "Oh, ages and ages."

Little Matt: "What about that time…"

The Brat: 'Shut up stupid. Don't say another word if you want to get laid ever again. Babes don't like guys who have been taken to the cleaners in divorce cases."

I decided that if "C" whoever he or she was had risked sending me two hundred clams, the least I could do was to meet him or her and hear what he or she had to say. I picked up the whole wad of papers and put them in my coat pocket as Caroline Adderley reentered my office preceded by the first female detective prospect.

CHAPTER THREE

WILSHIRE DISTRICT
LOS ANGELES
MOVEMBER 14, 1951
1:30 P.M.

In the negotiations leading to our cease fire agreement, one of the concessions I had wrung from Caroline Adderley before I surrendered my bloody, severed gonads to her as a trophy to put on her mantel at home, was to insist that I have the final say over who the agency hired and fired. For the past couple of months or so I had toyed with the idea of adding a female detective to the agency's roster of twenty-two males. (At one time I had over thirty detectives working for me, but a sudden epidemic of marital fidelity that swept Los Angeles in 1950 had necessitated the reduction of my work force.) My reasoning was that a woman gumshoe might be able to pry secrets out of other dames much easier than a man. Caroline Adderley had resisted the idea vehemently. The only women she had hired since she came to work for me were her assistant, Luann, and our receptionist, Betty. Both of these gals were timid and easy for

Caroline to push around. One would almost think that Caroline Adderley didn't like other women very much.

Caroline and I had finished interviewing three applicants by early afternoon. So far I hadn't liked what I saw. The first two women were matrons from the city jail. They were no nonsense ladies with eyes harder than the Hope Diamond. I couldn't see taking on either one because whichever one I hired would probably walk around slapping people just to get their attention before talking to them.

The third applicant was an ex policewoman from Philadelphia and was probably the ugliest woman I had seen in a long time. Fifty pounds overweight, she had little porcine eyes that darted around and couldn't make eye contact and an honest to goodness five o'clock shadow. This babe would go home alone from even the dimmest bar in Los Angeles on the day the world was scheduled to end. "She kinda looks a little like Humphrey Bogart. No, maybe two Humphrey Bogarts side by side," commented The Brat. This one was another definite no. I couldn't see anyone, even a blind woman, confiding secrets in her. When this applicant left the room I turned to Caroline.

"Whew," I commented, "how many more?"

"Just one, but I predict that you won't like her either," answered Caroline, as she left the room to go get the final prospective female detective. I had the interviewee's application in front of me. I looked it over as I waited. She had put down her name as Josephine Marx in bold, almost careless cursive, and she claimed to be twenty three years old. I scanned the list of questions she had answered on the application. Under a question asking for a listing of prior experience in detective related work, Miss Marx had answered, "None whatsoever, but how hard can it be to learn?" I figured from that answer that she was probably going to be another dud.

Even with my low expectations, I wasn't prepared for my first gander at the young lady when she walked in the door. She was of medium height and a tiny bit overweight, not fat mind you, but what the old guys out at the turkey farm would call pleasingly plump. Her short, pageboy style hair was uncombed and she wore no makeup, not even lipstick. She was dressed in a bulky sweater that was too large for her and dark wrinkled slacks. Despite all that, I could tell that if she were to doll herself up, she wouldn't look half bad. Miss Marx plopped herself down in the chair across from me and looked at me with an intense, challenging gaze. Caroline sat down in a chair beside the desk to my right.

"Young woman," said Caroline, speaking first, "Hasn't anyone ever schooled you on the proper attire for a job interview?"

Miss Marx turned her head toward Caroline and tilted her head back with a look that was the very picture of defiance. "If you want to know why I didn't make myself look pretty to impress you and this man here, I'll tell you. It's a travesty that women have to dress themselves in uncomfortable clothes and paint their faces and try to impress inconsiderate men in order to get ahead in today's society. Most women today are cowards and just go along with the charade, but not me!"

The Brat: "Oh, wow, you got yourself a man hater here. I wonder if she's also one of those Lesbinians we've heard about."

Captain Straight: "I think we're done here."

"Miss Marx, I detect a strong undercurrent of hostility towards men in your demeanor. Is it all men or just me that you're angry at?" I asked.

"Right now it's you. I was told to be here at nine for an interview. I was here on time because I'm a responsible person. You on the other hand amble in two hours late acting like the entitled jerk you probably are. And, no, I don't hate all men. My boyfriend Leopold isn't like you. He's a kind, gentle, considerate person who believes in equality of the sexes," said Miss Marx, boldly.

I glanced over at Caroline. She was trying to suppress a grin and acting like the cat that ate the canary.

The Brat: "I'd like to get a look at Leopold. I'll bet he's a real winner. She probably walks him around on a leash."

"Miss Marx, do you really want this job? It doesn't seem like you do. Insulting your prospective boss isn't the way to get hired," I said pretending to be stern.

"I just graduated college with a Bachelor's degree in criminology. I have set a goal for myself of being the first female Loa Angeles police chief. But the police won't hire me. I've applied three times. The last time I tried the sergeant that interviewed me said I was too 'Jewish' looking and that I should look for employment with a diamond merchant. I figure if I get some investigative experience under my belt, maybe they will give me a second look."

"So you want to be the chief of police, I should think that Chief Parker would have something to say about that," I replied.

"He's pretty old. By the time I make captain, he'll be long gone."

"Okay, is there anything else you would like to tell me?"

"Yes, as you have probably gathered from my answer a moment ago, I'm a Jew. If you have a problem with that we can just end this interview right now," said Miss Marx, with a squinty glare.

'Far from it. As a matter of fact one of my great-grandfathers was a Jew. So I have Jewish blood, too," I said, trying to engender feelings of camaraderie.

'Congratulations. I suppose now I'll have to show you our secret Hebrew handshake and tell you where we've got the world's gold stashed."

The Brat: "Hot damn, she sure knocked you flat with that crack. Even though she's a man hater, I'm starting to like this babe. She's as big a smartass as we are."

"Alright, Miss Marx, please have a seat out in the lobby. I have some things I have to discuss with my office manager. We'll call you back in when we're ready," I said pompously. Miss Marx eyed me skeptically but did as I requested and left the room.

"You're going to hire this nut aren't you?" asked Caroline when we were alone.

'What makes you think that?" I replied.

"Oh, I don't know. Maybe it's your affinity for screwballs, oddballs, nut cases and exotic people. Remember two years ago when you hired that dwarf and the first time he had to testify in court, Judge Rodriguez threatened to hold you in contempt for mocking him?"

"Is it my fault that Judge Rodriguez is only four-and-a-half feet tall and has a little man's complex? Walt Jenkins may have been small in stature but he was a good detective, you have to admit that. It was our loss when he got tired of taking insults and quit," I replied.

"Do I take all that as a yes? If so, do you want me to bring her back in now?" asked Caroline. I nodded.

When Miss Marx was again seated across from me I asked her if she had any further comments she would like to make before we announced our decision. Her defiant expression changed into a crestfallen look.

"You're going to reject me aren't you? I can tell, it happens to me a lot. Okay, let's get it over with," she replied.

"On the contrary, I'm prepared to hire you subject to two conditions. Number one, this job will require that you wear normal female attire. That includes skirts and frilly dresses as the occasion requires. Also, you will have to wear makeup and do up your hair. Do you think you can do that?" I asked.

As I told Miss Marx that I was prepared to hire her, a look of shock stole over the features of her face. She chewed her lower lip for a moment and then answered. "If that's a condition of employment, I guess it wouldn't compromise my principles. I would be like an army guy wearing a uniform. Yes, I think I could do that."

"Do you own any skirts or frilly dresses?"

"No, I don't and I'm damn proud of it," Miss Marx said. The defiant air was back.

"Okay, condition number two, I will be assigning you to one of my senior detectives to show you the ropes about how we do things around here. You will accompany him while he conducts his investigations. You must follow his lead and do what he tells you to do, at least for a while. Do you think you could do that?"

"I guess so, but being a man, anyone you put me with will eventually do or say something really stupid that will set me off. But I promise I will try to do what you ask."

Caroline then stood and took over in a very businesslike manner. "Miss Marx, if you'll follow me there is some paperwork you have to sign. Your salary will be exactly equal to what we pay our male probationary detectives. I will have my assistant, Luann, take you to the bullpen and introduce you to some of your fellow detectives." The bullpen was a huge room where the detectives all had their desks.

After the two women left and I was alone I called my wife at home.

"Hi, sugar, I have a favor to ask." I said when she came on the line.

"I'm open to just about anything except pushing another twelve pound baby through my pelvis. What do you want?"

"I have to work late tonight, probably till about eight or nine. Don't plug me when I come in the door late thinking I'm a prowler."

"It's okay. I knew when I married you that you work irregular hours. What is it this time?"

"I have to meet a client at a pro wrestling match," I said.

"Sounds like fun." I could tell she was being sarcastic.

"Aren't you worried that I'm lying to you and about to step out with a long legged brunette?"

"That's okay, if you feel the need to dally with a long legged brunette, go ahead. No one's stopping you. But I don't think you will enjoy being a eunuch. My mother told me once about how they used to castrate hogs on the farm when she was a girl. I'm sure she would be willing to hold you down while giving me step by step instructions."

All this talk about castration had a curious effect on Little Matt. He retreated up into some dark recess inside my body faster than the Silver Streak, dragging my scrotum with him. But my wife wasn't finished.

"You know, you being a eunuch will make my life so much easier. You will have to sit down to pee and you won't be able to hose down the bathroom walls with your urine like you do now. My question is how do you get it so high up on the wall. You'll have to show me sometime how you do it."

"It's all Little Matt's fault. He's always been a lousy shot."

"Well, I have to go now. Your son is yelling for his afternoon snack."

"Still love me?" I asked.

"Yes. Lord help me but I do, bye," she replied, and hung up.

As I hung up the receiver I heard a commotion outside in the main office. By the time I reached the hallway outside my door I could tell that the disturbance was coming from the bullpen. I could hear shouted angry voices. Caroline and I arrived at the bullpen at the same time. On one side of the room stood five or six angry detectives. One of them, John Priest, had a trickle of blood flowing down his upper lip from a nostril. On the other side of the room stood Miss Josephine Marx. She stood defiantly with a scowl and balled fists. I asked John what the hell was going on.

"I tripped over an open desk drawer and fell. I'll be okay," he replied. I could tell he was lying because I could see a red mark in the shape of a small hand on the side of his face that had the bleeding nostril. It wasn't hard for me to figure out what had happened. John Priest had said something unflattering and Miss Marx had coldcocked him.

'We need to talk," said Caroline, beside me. We went back to my office.

"Good luck with finding anyone willing to train Miss Marx. The way men talk, by the end of the day every detective will have heard about what happened."

I considered the situation for a moment then said, "I'll train her. Have her here at nine in the morning I'll be punctual this time. I promise."

I had another thought. "By the way, this afternoon have Luann get a hundred bucks from petty cash and take Miss Marx down to May Company. Tell your assistant to buy our new detective two outfits suitable for work. Just to be on the safe side, buy her underwear too. But don't get her any of those sheer panties you see advertised in magazines. Get her heavy cotton ones like they issue to the wonderful lady inmates up at Tehachapi Woman's State Prison."

"Okay," replied Caroline. "I'll bite. Why not buy her sheer panties?"

"If she should suddenly decide to sit cross legged like Tonto in the middle of Union Station, I don't want her to cause a scene and get arrested."

CHAPTER FOUR

DOWNTOWN
LOS ANGELES
NOVEMBER 14, 1951
7:05 P.M.

I didn't pull into the parking lot of the Olympic Auditorium until the first wrestling match of the evening had already started. The reason I was late was that I had stopped at the Pacific Dining Car on 6th Street near Witmer for dinner first. At this landmark Los Angeles restaurant, I dined on a perfectly cooked fillet mignon and consumed my daily allotment of three shots of Jack Daniels, Old No.7 bourbon. When I became a father I decided that I had to do something about my consumption of alcohol so I wouldn't set a bad example for my son as he was growing up. At the time Winston was born I was in the habit of carrying a pint bottle of bourbon with me wherever I went and walking around with a mild alcoholic buzz most of the time. I am proud to say that I have managed to moderate my drinking habit. I allow myself three alcoholic beverages after five o'clock and before dinner every night. Depending upon the day I have had, however, my drinks might be consumed when it's only five o'clock in places like Manilla or Ceylon.

The Olympic Auditorium was a huge white painted building standing at the corner of 18th Street and Grand Avenue. I had to circle around the parking lot for ten minutes before I found a place way in the back to park my Cadillac. I couldn't help but notice that there weren't many other fancy cars parked in the lot. They were mostly ten year old vintage Fords, Chevys and Plymouths. By the time I hobbled up to the front entrance of the auditorium after my trek across the parking lot, I felt like I had just finished the Long March with Chairman Mao. I bypassed the ticket booth and showed my ticket to an usher just inside the front door. As I waited for him to respond, I could hear the crowd roaring inside the place. The usher finally pointed me toward the east side of the auditorium and said my seat was ten rows back from the ring. He had to shout to be heard over the cheering and booing of the crowd inside.

The inside of the auditorium was laid out with a main floor that sloped gradually toward the center, where there was an elevated ring set up, guarded by ropes. Huge light, hung from the ceiling brightly illuminated the ring leaving the rest of the huge room in comparative gloom. Through the smoke from thousands of cigarettes, pipes and cigars, I saw that there was also a balcony that was sloped too, running all the way around the circumference of the auditorium. In a cleared area about six rows back from the ring on the west side there stood a large, boxy television camera with its operator behind it. "KTLA" was printed on both sides of the camera in big letters.

As I made my way to my seat, I examined the assemblage of people. The crowd that I would estimate at maybe two thousand people appeared to be overwhelmingly white and lower middle class. Very few suits, sport coats and ties were in evidence. The males in this bunch of people had opted instead for blue jeans, khaki work clothes and ball caps. The women in the crowd, as worked up as the men, were mostly dressed in slacks, pedal pushers, sweaters and other casual attire. They were on their feet and cheering or booing at two figures in the center of the ring.

Two enormously tall and fat men wearing garish colored tights were grappling with each other in the ring. One was face down on the mat with the other on top of him seemingly trying to twist his foot off his body. The guy on the bottom was striking the mat with his fists in agony and displaying elaborate facial expressions worthy of silent movie actress Theda Bara. Then, defying logic and probability, the wrestler on the bottom was suddenly on his feet. He grabbed the other guy and swung him up on his shoulders, turned in a circle several times and then slammed his burden down on the mat. The man on the ground just lay there stunned while his opponent back pedaled and used the ropes like a bow string to launch himself through the air and land on top of the guy on the ground with a splat. The referee darted in for a quick three count. Each number he called was accompanied by the swinging of his right arm down like he was holding a hammer. A loud bell clanged three times and the two huge wrestlers got to their feet with groans I could hear from my seat. A short pudgy guy wearing a checked sport coat and a bow tie climbed into the ring. I knew he was the announcer because he was holding a microphone the size of the Fifty Foot Woman's vibrator attached to a long wire. The announcer then began to interview the winner of the bout. The amplified conversation boomed throughout the cavernous building.

"Well, Crusher, how do you feel about your big win tonight?'

"I sure showed Gentleman Jim who was the best man here. It'll teach him not to go around shooting his mouth off about me," said Crusher in a voice that sounded like jigsaw cutting through a two-by-twelve. But Gentleman Jim was having none of that. He stomped over to the announcer in the checked coat and grabbed the microphone from his hand.

"I ain't gonna take them insults from you, Crusher. You only beat me cause I tripped. I demand a rematch! I'll be here a week from today to wrestle with you again. But then maybe you don't got the guts to face me," said Gentleman Jim. His voice was different from Crusher's. It sounded more like a hound dog dying of alcohol poisoning than a jigsaw. Crusher strode over to Gentleman Jim and snatched the microphone from his hand.

"I accept the challenge!" said Crusher and handed the microphone back to the announcer.

Captain Straight: "Oh, please, give me a break. I've heard more convincing dialog from Faye Wray when she was trapped in the big monkey's fist. "

"You heard the man folks," said the announcer enthusiastically." It sounds like we got a little feud going now between The Crusher and Gentleman Jim. If I was you I wouldn't miss next week for the world!"

While all this was going on, the wrestling fans in the crowd were all on their feet, baying like the hounds of hell. Most disdainers of the "sport" of pro wrestling couldn't understand why its fans got so worked up over something so obviously fake and contrived, but I knew why. If you worked for peanuts at some hard, physical job, you had an asshole boss and a nagging wife when you went home, you needed a place where you could yell out all your frustrations. If the truth were to be told these wrestling matches had probably saved the lives of countless asshole bosses and nagging wives.

The house lights came up as the occupants of the ring climbed over or through the ropes and made their way up an aisle. A lot of people in the crowd got up and started milling around near their seats while others streamed up the aisles headed for the restrooms or the concession stand.

The Brat: " Have you taken a good look at this crowd? Out of the couple thousand people here I bet there are only about nine hundred teeth distributed between them, including the ladies."

After about ten minutes the little announcer in the checked coat climbed back into the ring with his microphone and the house lights dimmed.

"Attention, ladies and gentlemen. For our second bout of the evening we have a real treat for you. Hold onto your hats when I announce the participants. In the northeast corner, the challenger, weighing in at three hundred and sixty pounds, IVAN, THE RED MENACE!" said the announcer, yelling out the last part and pointing toward the head of the north aisle. A spotlight snapped on and revealed a huge figure strutting down the aisle toward the ring. He was a gigantic man wearing bright red tights with a hammer and sickle communist emblem emblazoned across his chest and also a red cape of the same shade flowing out behind him. The man's hair was cut in a severe crew cut and had been peroxided a platinum blonde color. He was waving his arms above his head.

All of a sudden recognition dawned on me when I got a good look at his face and my jaw dropped. The man was none other than Carlo, the-mountain-and-a-half! I had last talked to Carlo about four years ago on the day that Bugsy Siegel had been murdered. At that time he was an enforcer for the Siegel-Cohen west coast mob. Two questions immediately came to mind. Number one, why was he passing himself off as a professional wrestler and, number two, what did he want with me.

Captain Straight: "My advice is for you to get up, leave the building and forget this. Nothing good is going to come of it, I feel it in my bones."

The Brat: "Oh I don't know. I'm kinda curious about his change of employment. It won't hurt to listen to what he has to say."

The crowd was immediately hostile to Carlo the mountain-and-a-half. A deafening chorus of boos erupted. As he neared the ring people started throwing wadded up programs and popcorn at him. The big man just grinned and swatted away the objects like King Kong swatting away biplanes atop the Empire State Building. Once inside the ring, Carlo stood quietly in his corner while the announcer once again strode to the center of the ring with his microphone.

"Ladies and gentlemen, in the southwest corner, the defender, weighing in at three forty, THE SARGE! This guy was almost as tall as Carlo but a shade smaller in stature. He wore olive drab tights with a pair of big, exaggerated sergeant's stripes on each arm, but no cape. On his head he wore a shiny G.I. helmet liner with another pair of stripes stenciled on the front. When he was introduced, the boos from the crowd were replaced with enthusiastic cheers.

The ensuing match, I have to say, was entertaining. There were plenty of Camel Clutches, Leg traps, Arm locks, Claw Holds, Head Scissors, Half and Full Nelsons, Chicken wings, Leg locks and Indian Death locks. Both wrestlers cooperated to put on a good show and make the fake combat appear, if not believable, at least plausible. The Sarge won the bout, but afterward there was no interview accompanied by amplified threats and bluster. As Carlo, in the guise of Ivan the Red Menace trudged dejectedly toward the exit, the crowd cheered themselves hoarse. They were thrilled that The Sarge representing the good old US of A had defeated the commie. After the bout I waited for about ten minutes and then went in search of dressing room G.

Asking an usher for directions to dressing room G, I was informed that all the dressing rooms for the wrestlers were in the basement. The usher directed me to a stairwell on the north side of the building that was being watched over by a bored guard. After bribing the rent-a-cop with a fin, I descended the stairs, walked down a dimly lit hallway that stank of stale sweat, cigar smoke and mold and found myself outside dressing room G. I knocked reasonably hard and pushed open the door.

Carlo the mountain-and-a-half was sprawled on his back atop a message table. He had a towel as big as a blanked wrapped around his huge lower body and a trainer was busily massaging his left calf. When he heard the door opening, Carlo turned his head and looked at me.

"Peeper! It was nice of you to come," he said holding out a hand as big as the states of California and Oregon combined. My hand disappeared in his and we shook.

"Carlo, nice to see you again. But you'll have to forgive me. I have a ton of questions. First and foremost, what the hell are you doing working as a professional wrestler and not a mafia torpedo?"

When I said this the trainer started and his ears perked up. Carlo looked at him. "Chuck, that'll be all. You can go." The man looked disappointed as he packed up his case of alcohol, tape and bandages and left. When we were alone, Carlo swung his legs over the side of the table and looked me in the eye for a moment before speaking.

"After Ben Siegel got bumped off, all hell broke loose between Siegel's New York crew and Jack Dragna's Chicago guys. Jack had always resented Ben Siegel for the way he had muscled in on his operations when he came to L.A. in 1938. With Siegel gone Dragna made his move. He tried to take over Ben's bookmaking and prostitution operations on all the west coast. Mickey Cohen, who had been Siegel's right hand man, wasn't having any of that. He fought back. Since that time the two of them have been trying like hell to bump each other off. Jack bombed Mickey's house and Mickey retaliated by mowing down three of Jack's guys with shotguns. Then Dragna attacked Cohen's headquarters at Sherry's Nightclub on Sunset with choppers, killing three of Mickey's guys." said Carlo. He wiped the sweat off his massive face with another towel and then continued.

"I had always thought that Ben Siegel was vicious, and he could be when he was riled. But he didn't hold a candle to Mickey Cohen. That guy would probably kill a waiter in a restaurant for forgetting to bring him a glass of water. One night he bumped off a member of his own crew with an ax in front of all of us. He did it because he said he had a hunch that the guy was spying for Dragna. Can you imagine that, killing a guy because you have a hunch? I started to get tired of all the tension in the life I was leading and started to look for a way out. Then about three years ago my chance came. One night I was driving while drunk and was stopped by a cop in Beverly Hills. When the cop searched me he found a forty-five automatic in a shoulder holster on me. Since

I had some minor felony convictions on my record, I was charged with being a felon in possession of a firearm and was sentenced to three years in Soledad Prison. I got out in eighteen months because of good behavior."

"When I got out of prison, I didn't go back to Mickey and tell him I wanted my old job back. Instead, I got a job loading trucks in a brickyard. I was a lot harder physically than being a gunsel, but I was content. Then one day a wrestling promoter stopped me on the street, handed me his card and asked me if I was interested in a new career. The rest is history."

"What about your cousin, Tony? He let you leave the family business just like that?" I asked.

"Tony's been dead since a couple of months after Siegel was rubbed out. One day he was yelling at some guys in the Flamingo Hotel and his ticker just gave out. He keeled over and died before anybody could get him to a hospital," replied Carlo.

"I'm sorry to hear that," I replied. But I was lying. I wasn't sorry. That bastard Tony Cardello had almost gotten me killed on more than one occasion. "Well, Carlo it's been nice to see you and all that, but you didn't contact me just to tell me about your wonderful new life. What do you want me to do for you?

"In my job as a wrestler I have to put up with a lot of yelling and noise. So on the nights I have a bout, I like to go down afterward to the Santa Monica pier late at night, walk out to the end and just enjoy the sound of the waves crashing on the beach. The air is clean and not full of smoke like in the Olympic."

"One night I noticed someone else on the pier doing the same thing I was, just enjoying the serenity. It was a good looking blonde dame with a knockout figure. I didn't approach her because why would a good looking woman like her want to talk to a big, ugly guy like me. But we kept running into each other there. Then one night about a couple of months after I first noticed her on the pier she came over to me, asked for a light for her cigarette and we started talking. Many nights after that we stayed until almost dawn just talking about life and feelings and crap like that. I didn't feel awkward with her and I sensed that she wasn't repulsed by my size and ugly mug. This is going to sound corny, but over time we fell in love. We even started talking about maybe someday getting married, living out in the country somewhere and having kids."

"She works as a chorus girl at the Havana nightclub on Sunset Boulevard in West Hollywood. Sometimes when the star singer is sick or something, she fills in for her. Her name is Daisy Carter, but at the club she calls herself Rhonda Faye. She came out here in forty-six to try her luck in Hollywood but like most girls that do that she didn't do too good. Well, the upshot is Daisy disappeared about a month ago. She just stopped meeting me on the pier like she always did. I went by her apartment a bunch of times but the place was always dark and nobody answered the door. She lives at the Carlton Arms Apartments on West Washington Boulevard, near Gramercy Place in Arlington Heights."

'Did you go to the Havana Club and try to find her there?" I asked.

"See, that's the thing," replied Carlo. "That's why I need you. I can't show my face at the Havana Club. The place is a hangout for most of the Dragna crew. If I was to show up there I'd stand out like a sore thumb because of my size and somebody might remember that I used to work for Ben Siegel and Mickey Cohen and figure I still did. They'd plug me on the spot. With the way things are right now between Mickey and Jack, it would be suicide for me to go there. Peeper, I need your help. Find Daisy for me. Even if something bad has happened to her, I want to know. I'll pay anything you ask. I've got plenty of dough right now. " When Carlo finished speaking the anguish was plain on his face.

I folded my arms, looked down at the floor and considered the proposition. Did I want to get involved again with gangsters? If I took this case it would be the third time I got myself dragged into the brutal world of the mob and almost got myself killed each time.

Captain Straight: "Don't say another word. Just turn around and leave."

The Brat: "This time I agree with the captain. Get the hell out of here and don't look back."

I swung my gaze back to Carlo's face intending to tell him I was refusing the case. But when I saw the hurt in his eyes I didn't have the heart to refuse him.

"Okay Carlo, I'll look into it," I replied.

CHAPTER FIVE

WILSHIRE DISTRICT
LOS ANGELES
NOVEMBER 15, 1951
9:30 A.M.

When I arrived at work I went into my private office, shucked my suit jacket, draped it over the back of my desk chair and fired up a Lucky Strike cigarette. Once I was seated I pressed a certain button on the intercom on top of my desk. "Betty, find Miss Marx and send her to my office," I said. "Yes, Mr. Cole," she replied.

About five minutes later my newest employee, Josephine Marx strode into my office. She was dressed in a tweed woman's business suit with a mid-calf hem, an open necked, cream colored blouse and flat heeled black shoes and was carrying a black leather purse by a strap over one shoulder. I was a little shocked to realize that she had a pretty good body after all. She was curvy in all the right places. The frumpy clothes she had worn to her interview had disguised it. Her short hair was neatly combed and she was wearing a muted shade of lipstick and a minimum of eye makeup. I was forced to admit that she was not a bad looking babe.

"Well, Miss Marx, how do you feel about starting your first day on the job?

"Aside from feeling embarrassed by having to wear this getup, I'm okay. But you'll never get me to wear high heels. They are just a gimmick designed to make a woman's calf look good to a lot of disgusting, leering men. If you try to get me to wear them, I won't do it," she replied in a firm tone with her arms crossed.

"Well, the first thing we need to get out of the way is what we will call each other," I said ignoring her ultimatum about high heeled shoes. "If we're going to be partners for a while we can't go around addressing each other as Mr. Cole and Miss Marx. What do your friends call you?"

"Miss Marx will do fine," she replied.

"Oh come on. What did your daddy call you when you were crawling around naked on the rug in front of the fireplace?"

"My father used to call me JoJo when I was little but I don't want you to call me that. I'm not a little girl anymore."

'Fine, JoJo it is. You can call me Matt." JoJo just rolled her eyes in disgust.

'You know, if you're not sure about this job, you can quit at any time," I said.

'You can't make me quit. You'll never be able to make me quit. You should just fire me right here and now and get this whole ridiculous charade over with," JoJo replied, with an angry look.

"Well. I'm not going to fire you. So if you won't quit, you have to do what I as your employer tell you to do. You can't take my money then not do the job. That would compromise those principles that you are so high and mighty about," I replied. I could tell by her expression that I had backed her into a corner and she wasn't happy about it. She gave me an angry nod.

"C'mon, JoJo, there are some things we have to do to get you equipped to be a detective," I said, as I put on my suit jacket and walked toward the door.

When we were seated in my old Ford work car, JoJo commented about the state of the interior. I have to admit that it was pretty bad. There was a coating of dust on the dash board, an overflowing ashtray as well as various items of trash including used paper coffee cups and candy wrappers littered the floorboards and the windshield was so dirty it looked like you were looking through the bottom of a Coke bottle.

"This car is filthy. It's a pig sty!" said JoJo.

"On the contrary," I replied. "The trash and the dust are carefully designed and fashioned camouflage. I had to work very hard to get it to this level of perfection." I replied.

"Uh-huh," she replied.

The first place we went was to a Sears & Roebuck department store. In the sporting goods section, I purchased a brand new Colt Detective Special revolver in .38 Special caliber, three boxes of ammunition and a cleaning kit in an oblong metal box. The bill came to $32.50 for the gun, $6 for the ammunition and $3.25 for the cleaning kit. Next, we drove to the LAPD academy pistol range in Elysian Park. It was where the police trained officers in firearms use, but the general public could also shoot there on a special side. I paid the fee and then set up the biggest target available in the range store about twenty-feet away from the firing line. I showed JoJo how to swing out the cylinder and load the revolver. I instructed her that this was a double action revolver. She didn't have to cock the hammer to fire but just pull the trigger through its cycle. I then told her how to use the sight on the gun and we stuffed balls of cotton in our ears. I pointed at the target and said, "Okay, fire away." As she raised the weapon in both hands, I stepped back and hid behind a concrete pillar.

The sound of six shots reverberated around the range. I emerged from behind the pillar, stood beside JoJo and looked at the target. She had missed the target completely with all six rounds. I listened for a moment for the sound of people yelling or the sirens of an ambulance rushing to treat a gunshot victim, but I didn't hear any. I told her to keep shooting.

The results were the same until she had worked her way through three quarters of a box of shells. Then, all of a sudden JoJo appeared to get the hang of shooting. She started to hit the target. By the time she was half way through the third box of shells most of her shots were grouping into a twelve inch circle surrounding the center bullseye with just a few strays. I limped up to JoJo to congratulate her. I saw that her face was a little flushed and her mood had improved. I could tell that she was enjoying herself.

"Maybe I should call you Annie Oakley instead of JoJo," I commented. For the first time that I had known her, she cracked a smile. Then it was instantly gone and the frown returned.

"It was hard at first, but then I realized the trick was the way I pulled back that trigger thingee. It got easier after that."

Our next stop was the Los Angeles Sheriff's headquarters on temple in downtown L.A. I found a place to park and we went inside where I helped JoJo fill out an application for a permit to carry a concealed weapon. I was careful to ensure that she wrote down the correct serial number of her new weapon.

The deputies in our esteemed sheriff's department were so bent; they rivalled Lincoln's first secretary of war, Simon Cameron, in corruption. Old Abe had once famously said of Cameron that "the only thing he won't steal is a red hot stove." The same could be said of the LASD so I wasn't surprised at what happened next.

When we turned in the application to a deputy at the desk, we were ushered into a small office containing a uniformed sheriff's sergeant seated behind a cluttered desk. His name tag identified him as Sgt. Morrison. He was about fifty with gray hair and a mustache and there must have been something wrong with his equilibrium because he leaned about thirty degrees to the left in his seat. I must have smiled because Morrison turned a little hostile. It wasn't my fault. I mean it's hard to take someone you're talking to seriously if they're listing like a freighter torpedoed by a U-boat.

The Brat: "The leaning tower of 210 West Temple Street."

The sergeant scanned JoJo's application then placed it in front of him on the desk.

"I'll take this under advisement. If you leave me a telephone number I'll call you in about six weeks, unless," he said then raised his eyebrows at me. I sighed, pulled out my wallet and threw two portraits of Andrew Jackson on top of the desk. The money disappeared into the sergeant's pocket as if by magic. Morrison nodded, took a small, stiff card from his right hand drawer, filled it out and handed it to JoJo. "Nice doing business with you," he said as we left.

When we were back in the car and headed back to my office, JoJo asked me, "Is everyone in government in Los Angeles as corrupt as that?"

"The sheriff has been on Jack Dragna's payroll for years. An organization rots from the top. The police department is not much better. About a third of LAPD officers take bribes from Mickey Cohen, another third from Jack Dragna and the remaining third are honest guys just trying to do a decent job. However, we have a police chief now that's trying to clean up the department and throw out all the crooked cops. Let's hope he succeeds."

I parked my old car in its slot at my office and turned to JoJo. "That's enough for your first day. You can go home and clean your revolver and practice your fast draw in front of a mirror. Just remember to unload the gun first. By the way, it would be a definite violation of your principles, as well as highly illegal, if you were to lose your temper and shoot your boss with your new gun."

"Oh, I don't know, I might make an exception in your case," said JoJo with another fleeting smile as she got out of the car. As I watched her walk away, my stomach rumbled and I realized that I was very hungry. I glanced at my watch and saw that it was a few minutes past one in the afternoon. I decided to go to my office, check for messages then maybe go out somewhere nice for a late lunch. As I limped up to Betty's counter in the lobby, she did what she always did; she shot up straighter from a slouch and greeted me. "Good afternoon Mr. Cole."

"Hello Betty, anything going on?" I asked her.

"Yes sir. There is a gentleman from the police in the waiting room who says he needs to talk to you." I turned to look just as a man stood from one of our hard as rocks sofas and took off his gray felt fedora. I recognized him right away.

The years since 1944 appeared to have been good for Detective Sergeant Miller of the LAPD. His hair wasn't any grayer or his jowly face any more hangdog than he was when he was the investigating sergeant of a murder that I was being framed for but didn't commit. In fact, he looked much more rested than the last time I had seen him. I ambled over to Miller and we shook hands.

"Well Sergeant Miller, it's been a long time. Apparently you want to talk to me. Would it behoove me to have a lawyer present during this little chat?"

"Well, first off, it's Lieutenant Miller now. I work a special detail out of the chief's office. You're not in any trouble. I just need you to accompany me somewhere for about an hour. Someone I know wants to talk to you. Afterward you will be free to go and I won't bother you again."

"Where would we be going and who is it you want me to meet?" I asked.

"I can't tell you either of those things," replied Miller with a wry smile.

Captain Straight: "Pardon me while I turn down the clanging alarm bells and switch off the flashing red warning lights. A cop shows up here, says he wants you to go and meet some mysterious someone and won't tell you who it is or where you're going is not a good sign. My advice to you is to turn around and go call your shyster right now."

The Brat: "I agree, going with this cop would not be smart."

My long term tormentors were probably right. It wouldn't be smart to go with Miller. But since when have I not done stupid things on occasion. In fact I was the California champion of acting stupid. I had fallen for the glib talk of a Marine recruiter and ended up half crippled with voices constantly jabbering away in my head. I had allowed a phony lawyer to frame me for a murder I hadn't committed and I had allowed myself to get involved with the Siegel/Cohen gangster crew on more than one occasion. I would venture to say that if you were to add up all the dumb things I have done in my life and put them in a big bag, it would far outweigh a similar bagful of the times I acted smart. Miller was an honest cop and a straight shooter who had treated me fairly in the past, so I trusted him. But the real reason I was inclined to accompany Lieutenant Miller was my curiosity as to who this mysterious person was, who wanted to talk to me.

"Okay, Lieutenant Miller, lead on," I replied.

The lieutenant's car was parked on Wilshire in front of my office. It was an unmarked 1950 Ford, Fairlane sedan painted black and it was parked in a red, bus zone. Miller had used the cop trick of draping the radio microphone and cord over the rear view mirror so the parking control officers would know it was a police car and not put a parking ticket under the windshield wiper. We got in and Miller drove us over to Chinatown and stopped in front of the Celestial Kingdom Chinese Restaurant on N. Broadway near Spring Street. Instead of parking in front of the place, though there were plenty of spaces available on Broadway, he turned down an alley and parked in the back of the restaurant by the kitchen door. Throughout the drive Miller had remained silent.

We entered through the kitchen door and our noses were assaulted by a mixture of delicious aromas. Having not eaten since the morning, my mouth started to water involuntarily. The Chinese cooks and waiters, all chattering away in Mandarin, paid us no attention as we walked through the kitchen and up a flight of stairs to a private room off a narrow hallway. The lieutenant ushered me inside.

The room was about fifteen feet square and was decorated with murals on two of the walls. One was a representation of the Great Wall of China. The other was of two dragons breathing fire on each other in flight. Three tables occupied the floor space of the room, enough to seat a party of about twenty people. All of the tables were empty save one. Its sole occupant was a dour looking man in a suit that might have worn by an undertaker at a funeral, all black except for a white shirt. He appeared to be in his late forties with a medium build, receding dark brown hair and glasses. Vertical creases in his cheeks framed a mouth set in a stern, hard line and his eyes looked at me with an intense, unwavering gaze. The man looked very familiar and I felt that I should know him but I couldn't quite remember where I had seen that face.

Lieutenant Miller stepped from behind me as we approached the seated figure. "Matt Cole," said Miller, "meet William Parker, Chief of Police of the City of Los Angeles." I froze in surprise. What the hell did the chief of police want with me?

CHAPTER SIX

CHINATOWN
LOS ANGELES
NOVEMBER 15, 1951
2:10 P.M.

"**M**r. Cole, nice to meet you," said the chief and then extended his hand. He wasn't smiling. I wondered if he had ever smiled in his life. We shook hands and then Chief Parker motioned to a chair across the table from where he was sitting. "Please be seated."

I did as he asked. Chief Parker was still staring at me intently like he could discern something about me by my appearance. I noticed that Parker's back was ramrod straight, like he was sitting at attention in his chair.

The Brat: "Maybe he's got a nightstick shoved up his ass. That would explain the pained look."

"Mr. Cole," began Parker, "I have an important matter to discuss with you but I have some questions first if you don't mind."

"Go ahead," I answered.

"It is the opinion of the men in my intelligence division as well as the word on the street that you are somehow tied in to Mickey Cohen and his group of New York based criminals. However, Lieutenant Miller here has vouched for you. He says that when you were a policeman you were one of the honest ones and that if you associated with Siegel or Cohen it was against your will. Which is it?"

"Wait a minute here," I replied, starting to get very annoyed. "What are you trying to accuse me of? Maybe I should just leave right now and contact my lawyer."

"Please, Mr. Cole, just answer the question. It's very important."

"Okay," I replied, "I have been dragged into the west coast mob's sphere twice in the past seven years. The first time was in 1944. A guy pretending to be a lawyer set me up to take the fall for the murder of one of Siegel and Cohen's betting parlor managers. I spent the night in jail and the next day the fact that I was a suspect was all over the front page of the Times. It also turned out that the murdered guy had over fifty grand of the mob's money on him when he was bumped off and this money was missing. Mickey Cohen had me snatched the day I was let out of jail. Instead of killing me, Mickey gave me ten days to recover the money. I solved the murder and returned the money to the mob."

"Did you get a cut of the money?" asked the chief.

"Mickey Cohen gave me a thousand dollars as a reward and believe you me, I earned every penny of it." I replied.

"Alright, what about the second time you were involved with them?"

In 1947 Tony Cardello, a pit boss at the Mob's Flamingo Hotel in Las Vegas, who I had met the first time I got sucked into the mob's orbit, hired me to find his missing sister who was last seen at Bugsy Siegel's Beverly Hills mansion. I didn't want to take the case but Tony leaned on me to do it, intimating that it wouldn't be healthy for me to refuse. A day or two later, Virginia Hill, Bugsy's longtime girlfriend also hired me to find a missing diamond bracelet. I did my job. I found the bracelet and the sister and that was that," I said. I left out the part about the involvement of Carlo, the mountain-and-a-half. It was none of Parker's business and the fact that Carlo was also a present client would be too hard to explain.

Were you anywhere near the Siegel mansion when he was murdered?" asked the chief.

'I don't want to talk about any of that. I had to do a boat load of fancy maneuvering to stay alive during that time. Let's just let those sleeping dogs lie."

"We could arrest you and make you talk," said Parker.

"Well Chief, you could do that but I wouldn't advise it. You know, my father died a few years ago and left me over two million dollars. The ne'er do well brother of my father's long-term live in companion contested the will. On my father's lawyer's recommendation I hired the law firm of Madison, Madison, Simon and Cheeseman. I won the case because these lawyers are so good that if Adolph Hitler had hired them instead of killing himself, he not only would have been cleared of starting World war Two, but they could also have gotten him elected mayor of Santa Monica. I think we're done here," I said and started to rise from my chair.

"Please, Mr. Cole," said Chief Parker as he relaxed a little and leaned back in his chair. "I'm satisfied that you are not affiliated with these mobsters. Please stay a while longer. I have a proposition for you."

"Well, okay. What the hell is this all about anyway?"

"I have been a Los Angeles police officer for twenty-four years. During those years I had to witness blatant corruption of my fellow officers on a daily basis. It made me angry but what could I do about it? The answer was nothing. Then last year, thanks to a reform minded mayor, I was appointed police chief and I gained the opportunity to do something about crooked cops. I am determined to clean up the Los Angeles Police Department and make it a shining example to other law enforcement agencies around the country of a corruption free, efficient and ethical police agency," said Parker, and paused for a moment while he gathered his thoughts. Then he continued.

"I have been chief for a little over fifteen months. During that time I have managed to drive the dirty cops out of most of the divisions within the department. I'm not a fool. I know that I won't be able to stop all petty corruption like beat cops accepting free meals and smokes from merchants, but I can stop cops from accepting bribes from organized crime, running protection rackets and other serious violations of their sworn duty. As I said, I have had some success but one division has been a thorn in my side."

"The Vice Division is commanded by Captain Brian Reed. Captain Reed is totally corrupt and has been on Jack Dragna's payroll since 1937. He routinely deploys vice officers to protect and facilitate Dragna's gambling and prostitution operations. The problem is that Reed is being protected by certain members of the City Council. A little over a month ago, thinking I had the votes in the council, I made my move to get rid of Captain Reed. The mayor made a motion in a regularly scheduled meeting to demote Captain Reed to sergeant and transfer him to the Harbor Patrol. At the last minute, Councilman Conrad, who we thought we could count on, abruptly switched his vote to oppose us. My suspicion is that either Dragna or Reed got to Conrad using bribery or threats and made him change his vote," said Chief Parker.

"This is all very interesting. You should write a screenplay and pitch it to a movie studio. But for the life of me I can't understand where I come in on any of this," I replied.

"Bear with me for just a moment and I'll tell you," said the chief testily.

The Brat: "We're gonna starve to death before this son of a bitch comes to the point."

Captain Straight: "Hush! This is interesting. I want to hear what he says."

"The war between Jack Dragna and Mickey Cohen is going decidedly in Cohen's favor. I have it on good authority from sources that I am not at liberty to name that Captain Reed of the vice division is interested in switching his allegiance from Dragna to Cohen. But because of the state of relations between the two gangs he has no way to contact Cohen to make his pitch. Each faction is so paranoid now that anyone from the other side approaching them is shot on sight."

"What I propose is that we put a bee in the ear of some people close to Reed intimating that you are an in to the Cohen gang. Your past associations with them will lend credence to the rumors. Sometime this week, we will arrange for your personal automobile to be picked up and taken to a certain garage for an oil change. While your vehicle is in the garage, a technician from my intelligence division will install a hidden microphone attached to a wire recorder powered by your vehicle battery, with a secret button under your dashboard that activates the recorder. Certain other locations around the city will also be wired and we will tell you where they are in specific detail. When or if you are approached by Captain Reed or one of his underlings, your job will be to maneuver the meeting place within range of one of these microphones and record their pitch."

"You know that secret recordings might not stand up in court, right?" I said.

"I have no intention of prosecuting Captain Reed," replied Parker. "I want to focus so much public heat on him that he will just retire and go away. Once he is gone I will make short work of his underlings. I have primed two newspaper reporters, one with the Times and the other with the Examiner to run banner stories about Reed's corruption after you have provided some proof," said the chief. After he paused for a moment or two, he continued. "I guess we're down to brass tacks. I can't pay you anything tangible or intangible for your service. If you do what I ask, the only remuneration you will receive will be that you know that you are participating in a righteous cause. Will you do it?"

I sat back in my chair, bowed my head and studied my nails while I reflected on Chief Parker's proposal. There was a big element of risk for me if I accepted. A hundred things could go wrong resulting in me being chopped up in little pieces and fed to the fish in Santa Monica bay. I was a husband and father now and shouldn't take risks like this one.

Captain Straight: "You're right, Matt. Doing what he asks will be very risky. Maybe you should sleep on it before deciding."

The Brat: "Screw this guy. What has the police department ever done for you? When you came back from the war hurt and tried to get your job back they threw you away like a piece of trash. You don't owe them anything."

I sat up straight, looked Chief Parker in the eye and said, "Okay, I'm in."

"Speaking for the department and myself, I wish to thank you for your willingness to serve," replied the chief.

'I'm not doing this for you or even the department. I'm doing it for the honest cops out there who come to work every day and try to do a hard, thankless job and maybe help someone in the process. They don't deserve to be tarred with the same brush as the crooks they are forced to work with," I replied.

CHAPTER SEVEN

FAIRFAX DISTRICT
LOS ANGELES
NOVEMBER 16, 1951
9:00 A.M.

J ust before I left my house, stuffed with food, June intercepted me at the door and gave me a kiss. It wasn't one of those perfunctory pecks on the cheek either, but a full on the lips barnburner. When she stepped back afterward she displayed that moist eyed, intense expression on her face that I had come to know very well since our wedding. It was lust. I knew that later that night, after Winston was asleep, my beautiful wife would bound into our bedroom without a leap in between, tear my pajamas off and commit a violent but wonderful sexual assault on my body. Little Matt stirred as he did anytime sex was discussed, and started to rise with excitement.

The Brat: "Whoa there, stupid, you're about sixteen hours too early. Just go back to sleep and we'll let you know when it's time for you to go into your hysterics."

Little Matt: "Sixteen hours? Then why the hell is everybody talking about it now and getting me all excited for nothing?"

Winston, who was nestled on my wife's right hip wearing nothing but a cloth diaper and apparently disgusted by our display of affection suddenly grabbed June's right breast possessively. He then gave me a petulant glare similar to the one I'm sure he displayed when he ordered the Royal Navy to destroy the French fleet at Mers El Kebir. I interpreted his expression as a warning. "These are mine," he was telling me non-verbally. "Keep your cotton picking hands off them until all the milk is gone."

I considered driving to work in my new Cadillac, to be the best part of my daily routine. Today was no exception. It was after nine, so the morning rush hour was over. Consequently the traffic was light. Los Angeles had gained population spectacularly since the war, but it was still a grand place to live. The November morning air was crisp and not too full of smog yet. The ride of my car was smooth. Even when I went over the bigger potholes my Cadillac's gazillion mechanical parts all functioned flawlessly together, giving me a feeling that all was right with the world. Then I went and spoiled it all by turning on the radio and tuning it to station KRLA for the morning news.

"... spokesman for Coco Chanel has announced that women's hemlines for 1952 will remain at mid-calf," said the radio announcer. "In other news from Korea, because of the resumption of peace talks at Panmunjom, General Ridgeway has announced that he has ordered U.N. forces to cease major offensive operations and assume a static defense. And now a word from our sponsor. Do you feel listless and tired by mid-morning? If you do, you should try Wheaties, the breakfast of champions. The combination of vitamins and minerals in Wheaties will give you new pep and vigor. . ." I reached over and switched off the radio.

I thought the news from Korea was screwy. I couldn't imagine General Eisenhower announcing in 1944 that he was going to cease chewing up the German Army in France because the Nazis might possibly be amenable to a negotiated peace. I bet that if Eisenhower gave George Patton that order, Georgie would have mutinied and lead his Third Army across the channel in a reverse D-Day and hung Ike as a traitor from the nearest London lamp post. But then again, Korea was a screwy war. During World War Two, Americans had followed the progress of the war closely, many with war maps on their walls at home. The conflict was the general topic of conversation in barber shops, at the country club and wherever Americans gathered. Korea was different. Nobody seemed to want to talk about it. It was like if they didn't discuss it, the whole nasty little war would go away. The only people who seemed to care were the loved ones of the soldiers and Marines doing the fighting. But the young members of the armed forces who managed to survive and come back home in one piece would have learned a valuable lesson: Believing what gas-bag politicians tell you can very often get you maimed or killed.

When I limped into the lobby of my detective agency, I was confronted by Caroline Adderley and JoJo Marx standing side by side at Betty's counter with their arms folded and both with looks of disapproval. Caroline looked the way she always did, like a sinister spinster headmistress of an English school for girls. The only thing that was missing was a two-foot long ruler with which to whack the knuckles of wayward young ladies. JoJo on the other hand looked pretty good. She was wearing the second of the two outfits we had bought her. This one was a lime green woman's business suit with a cut that emphasized the curves of her figure. It also looked like she had taken more care with her hair and makeup than yesterday. Without a hello or anything, JoJo piped right up.

"Mrs. Adderley told me yesterday that it was very important for me to be here at 8:30. She emphasized that in this office, punctuality is a virtue adhered to by all. But for the second time in three days you have kept everyone waiting. Maybe I should have brought a copy of Reader's Digest with me today just to occupy my time while waiting for you."

"Don't even try honey," interjected Caroline. "I've been trying to get him here on time for years and nothing has worked. You might as well save your breath."

"Don't call me honey," replied JoJo.

"You're right ladies; I'm late and I have no legitimate excuse. And as the boss around here I'm not going to stand for this breach of office rules. I'm gonna do something about it. I'm gonna go into my private office, light up a cigarette and give myself a severe tongue lashing."

"Oh, men!" JoJo said loudly as we parted, all going in different directions like we were breaking up from a football huddle.

"Oh, Mr. Cole," said Betty the receptionist. "A Lieutenant Miller called and left a kind of cryptic message for you. He said that you were to leave your Cadillac car keys with me and a mechanic from the Pep Boys garage would come and pick up the car and perform the modification he had discussed with you. He also said that he would leave a packet with some locations on the front seat Do you know about this or was it just a prank call?"

"Yeah, it's legit," I told her and handed over my keys. Next, I went into my private office and retrieved my gun from the locked lower drawer of my desk. It was a large Colt Government Model pistol in a soft leather holster that I stuffed inside my waistband at the small of my back and clipped to my belt. Next, I broke off a small portion of modeling clay from the fair sized brick of the stuff I kept in a filing cabinet and put it in a coat pocket. Leaving my office I went to the bull pen and retrieved JoJo. She was sitting at a desk in the corner, looking out a window and fuming.

"C'mon kid, let's get going. We're burning daylight," I said to her. She rolled her eyes toward the ceiling.

"Said the man who was an hour late to work, and don't call me kid."

"You know you can quit anytime you want," I replied.

"Never!"

We took the elevator down to street level and got in my old, dusty Ford work car. As I drove out of the parking lot and turned west on Wilshire, JoJo asked me where we were going. Without telling her many details or the back story, I told her about the case of Carlo the mountain-and-a-half's missing girlfriend. Our first stop would be the dame's apartment house.

"When we get there, don't say anything. Let me do the talking," I told Jo-jo. "By the way, yesterday afternoon, when you went home did you show your parents your new gun?"

"I didn't go straight home yesterday. I went back to that pistol range and did some more shooting. I met a cop named Leonard there who gave me some better pointers than you did on my shooting. He works at night in Hollenbeck division. We're going to meet there at the range again this weekend and he's going to bring his forty-five with him to see if I can handle it."

The Brat: "So he's gonna bring his forty-five to see if she can handle it is he? Is that what young cops are calling their Johnsons these days. Tell her not to be disappointed when his forty-five turns out to be a twenty-two."

"What about you boyfriend, Leopold. Isn't he gonna be jealous of you meeting with a handsome young officer and fondling guns with him while you look into each other's eyes?" I asked, ignoring The Brat's remark.

"No, Leopold is different from the rest of you men. He believes in the equality of the sexes. He never tries to tell me who I can see or what to do."

There was an empty parking spot on West Washington Boulevard in front of the Carlton Arms Apartments and I deftly slipped my old Ford into it. The building was a three story pinkish brown stucco structure with phony attachments on its front face to make it resemble an English country house. We got out of the Ford and entered the lobby of the building. Once inside, I looked at the bank of mailboxes to see what name Carlo's girlfriend had given the building management. Next to the label for apartment 2C was a white card in a slot with the handwritten notation

"D. Carter." Leading Jo-jo down the central first floor corridor, I stopped at a door that had sign over it that read "Building Manager" and knocked.

The man who answered the door was about sixty, with a bald head, gray mustache and thick glasses. He was wearing brown pants pulled up to his armpits and held up with suspenders underneath a rumpled brown sweater. I could detect crumbs in his mustache. We must have interrupted his lunch or mid-morning snack.

'Yes," he said in a somewhat feeble voice. "My name's Hilton. How can I help you folks?"

"Yes, Mr. Hilton, the missus and I were just driving by and we decided to drop in and inquire about an apartment. We have always admired your building and since I just got a big promotion, we can now afford to live here," I said as folksy as I could.

"Well, you folks might be in luck. I got a tenant that has disappeared. She just walked out one day about a month ago and didn't come back. I was planning to put her stuff down in the basement the first of next month when her rent becomes due and rent out her apartment to someone else. By the way, I didn't catch your name."

'My name is Pringle, Eldon Pringle. This is my wife Leticia," I said, as I shook hands with Hilton. As the old guy stepped forward to shake hands with JoJo but before he could grasp her hand I moved in close and said in a stage whisper that could have been heard down the block, "I wouldn't shake the little woman's hand today mister. She had a strange rash on her lady parts this morning."

Hilton's hand dropped quicker than Johnstown real estate after the flood. I glanced at JoJo. She was red in the face and giving me a glare exactly like the one seen on Cain's face as he looked at his brother Abel just before the first murder.

"If it wouldn't be an inconvenience, could we take a look at the apartment? "I asked.

"Don't see why not. Let me get my passkey." Hilton disappeared inside his apartment and returned momentarily with a key attached to a long red ribbon which he put in his right sweater pocket. He led us slowly upstairs to apartment 2C, unlocked the door with his passkey and returned it to the sweater pocket then ushered JoJo and I inside. He stood near the door while we wandered around.

It was a small apartment consisting of a good sized living room, kitchenette, bedroom and a small bathroom. It was decorated with furniture in the modern style. All the tables and other wood pieces in the apartment were made out of maple wood and generally consisted of what looked like slabs of wood supported by spindly, round tapered legs. A floral print sofa and two chairs were positioned around a tall radio cabinet made out of what appeared to be mahogany. All in all, the furniture gave the impression of being of good quality and also looked expensive, much too expensive for a chorus girl making sixty bucks a week. I maneuvered JoJo into the bathroom and whispered to her, "Go in and stand beside Hilton and pretend to faint."

"You Jerk, after that crack about the rash, why should I do anything for you?" she whispered back.

"Does this mean you're quitting your job?" I asked still whispering.

"No!" she answered and with a pert toss of her head, walked into the living room toward Mr. Hilton. As she approached the old guy, JoJo suddenly staggered, put the back of her left hand to her forehead and said in an imitation Scarlet O'Hara southern voice, "Oh dear, ah fear ahm about to faint." With that she collapsed into Hilton's arms, but instead of catching her, the old guy stood back and JoJo hit the carpeted floor with a clunk. "Are you alright Ma'am?" asked Hilton as he got to his knees beside JoJo and as I rushed over. While Hilton was distracted and frantically patting the backs of JoJo's hands, I reached into his sweater pocket and retrieved the pass key. Quickly removing the ball of clay from my pocket, I pressed each side of the key into the clay and returned it to Hilton's pocket in under four seconds.

As I was helping JoJo to her feet I said, "don't mind Leticia, she does this all the time. Whenever she has her monthly cycle she gets kind of unsteady. She gets moody and irritable too" We made our escape quickly after that. I thanked Mr. Hilton and told him that I would check back with him around the first of the month.

'You know, you're a bastard," said JoJo when we were back in the car. Then, not waiting for a response, she asked me why I had asked her to do the fainting act. "Because I want to come back here later and search that apartment. It will be easier to enter with a key than to pick the lock." I then showed her the ball of clay with the impressions of both sides of the key embedded in it.

"Being around you all morning, maybe I should check and see if I still have my wallet in my purse," she said, sarcastically.

"You did well in there. You passed your first test," I said to her. She acted indifferent to the compliment but I suspected that she was secretly pleased and excited. I could tell by her flushed face and throbbing of a vein in her neck.

"Did you see that old geezer let me fall to the floor like that?" asked my partner.

"Yeah, but it was so much more convincing the way it happened." I replied.

I drove to Jack's Lock and Key on San Pedro Street near Jefferson. It was a rundown place with a layer of dust on every horizontal surface. Jack himself was behind the counter when we entered. He was about fifty with a long narrow face and small eyes that were never still, but darted all over the place nervously like a drum majorette in a parade who couldn't remember if she put on her panties that morning. As I lay the ball of clay with the impressions and a twenty-dollar bill on top of the counter, Jack shook his head.

"As I told you last time, I can't do any more keys from impressions. I could get in a lot of trouble for doing that," he said frowning. I sighed, took out my wallet and laid another twenty on the counter. Jack hesitated for a moment, then nodded, picked up the money and the ball of clay and disappeared into his backroom. Twenty minutes later as we left Jack's in possession of an illegal pass key for the Carlton Arms Apartments I was grumbling to myself that Congress should to do something about the rampant inflation in the country. The price of an illegal key had doubled in the last six months.

After lunch at Pinks hot dog stand, JoJo and I spent the afternoon working on various routine cases that Caroline Adderley had assigned to me. Most were divorce cases. Two and a half hours of our time was spent at the Hall of Records searching through dusty old business records and property deeds. It was all very boring and I caught JoJo yawning several times.

When I pulled my old Ford into its slot in front of my office at five o'clock, I told JoJo, "Don't come in to the office on Monday until two in the afternoon. We have some night work to do."

"But I have a date Monday night with Leopold. We're going to go to Music City. Doris Day is going to be there and introduce a new song. I can't work late with you," she replied.

"Do I interpret that answer to mean that you're quitting?" I asked.

"Hell no!" replied JoJo before she wrenched open the passenger door and angrily slammed it shut after getting out.

CHAPTER EIGHT

WILSHIRE DISTRICT
LOS ANGELES
NOVEMBER 19, 1951
2:10 P.M.

C aroline Adderley met me when I first entered the office. She had a concerned look on her face.

"Peter Adams just got burned on a surveillance. It's the Detweiller case," said Caroline. Peter Adams was one of the firm's detectives but I wasn't familiar with this particular case. When I gave Caroline a blank look, she explained further. "It's a standard husband infidelity case. The wife thinks he is stepping out on her with his secretary. Peter erred and got too close and he's sure that Detweiller spotted him. He felt that the best thing to do was to back off and return to the office. The bullpen is empty. Everyone else out of the office working on their own cases. Can you and Miss 'Hard case' follow Detweiller for the rest of the day?" I considered her request. In actuality, much of what I had to do that evening couldn't be accomplished before dark anyway.

"Sure, I think we can handle that," I said. Caroline looked relieved. "Is JoJo here?" I asked.

"She's sitting in the kitchen and let me warn you, she doesn't look happy. I'll get you the fact sheet on the Detweiller case and you can pick it up at Betty's desk when you go out."

I went toward a small room next to the bullpen. We called it the kitchen but there wasn't a stove or hotplate or utensils to cook anything. Inside, there was a round table, four hard chairs and a big urn of coffee that we kept simmering throughout the day. By the end of the workday, the stuff tasted like sludge from a truck's crankcase.

JoJo was sitting in one of the chairs at the table with a cup of coffee in front of her. From the expression on her face, I assumed that she was in a particularly surly mood. She had on a white blouse, pink sweater and dark full skirt instead of one of the outfits we bought her. She must have had some presentable clothes at home that she hadn't told us about.

"Well, I'm surprised," she said when she looked up at me. "I figured that I would have to sit here a couple of hours more before you showed up."

"You okay?" I asked.

"Sure, I'm just peachy," she replied, as she got up and slung her black purse over her shoulder. She followed me out to the

Ford and we got in. Before starting the car I scanned the fact sheet on the Detweiller case.

"Okay, before we work on our own cases, we have to help another detective on one of his," I said. "The target is a well-off businessman named Detweiller. His wife suspects that ole' Detweiller is doing a little more than dictating letters to his pretty young secretary. He is an executive with the J.T. Mantz Company. Their office is on 6th Street near Main. We're going to drive over there, locate Detweiller's car, find a good vantage point and see what transpires."

"How come we have to do somebody else's work?" asked JoJo.

'It's what we do in this line of work; we cooperate," I answered. She looked like she wanted to make a further comment but then apparently thought better of it and remained silent throughout the drive over to 6th and Main.

When I pulled into the parking lot for the Mantz Company I again consulted the case fact sheet and started looking for Detweiller's car. I found it parked in the first row of stalls, which made sense. Detweiller was an executive so he would have a reserved space close to the building. The car was a late model Cadillac, like mine but bigger, with four doors. It was painted maroon. Next, I looked for a spot to park my Ford that would allow me an unobstructed view of Detweiller's car. Unfortunately, the only spot available that fit the criteria was much too close, only about fifty feet away from the target's Cadillac. Well, beggars can't be choosers I thought and parked in the spot.

I glanced at my watch. It was 2:35 p.m. I fidgeted in my seat to make myself as comfortable as possible while we waited. After a few minutes, JoJo looked over at me.

"So what happens now?" she asked.

"We wait. You'll soon find out that a good part of a detective's day is spent waiting. So relax but stay alert. This guy might not emerge from the building until after five or he could come out within the next five minutes. I sometimes bring crossword puzzles with me or listen to the radio; anything to make the time go faster."

"Well this is boring," she commented, as she fanned away the smoke from my burning cigarette.

"We could talk to help pass the time. How's Leopold?" I asked.

"Leopold fooled me. I thought he believed in true equality of the sexes, but he turned out to be just like the rest of you men. This past weekend, I told him about getting a gun and a permit to carry it concealed. He blew up and said that he wasn't comfortable dating a woman who carried around a lethal weapon. Can you believe he gave me an ultimatum? He said that either I get rid of the gun or our relationship is over."

The Brat: "Sounds like maybe we sold Leopold short. Maybe he's smarter than we gave him credit for."

"Maybe he'll be back after he's thought it over," I said.

"I wouldn't take him back now if he showed up at my door carrying two cute puppies with bows around their scrawny little necks and offering a bonus of a subscription to National Geographic Magazine. Hey, wait a minute, why am I telling you any of this? It's none of your damn business," replied JoJo hotly and clammed up.

At around three-thirty a well-dressed man in his fifties with white hair emerged from the building and walked cautiously toward the parking lot. I glanced at the photograph of the target paper clipped to the fact sheet. The man was Detweiller.

He stopped beside his Cadillac and began surveying the parking lot. I became nervous that we would be spotted because we were so close to him.

"Quick, pretend to kiss me," I told JoJo.

"What?" she asked incredulously?

"The target's spooked and looking all around. If he spots us we'll be blown," I said quickly.

JoJo launched herself into my arms, encircling my neck with her own arms and crushed her lips against mine. And this wasn't an antiseptic, closed mouth kiss, but one with lips parted like Rhett Butler gave Scarlet O'Hara outside a burning Atlanta. He lips were soft and yielding. Little Matt took off and climbed like a spad intercepting a fokker. As surprised as I was, I still kept an eye on Detweiller. He saw us and his eyes dwelt on us for a moment then moved on. Apparently satisfied, the target got in his car.

JoJo broke the kiss and acted as if nothing had happened.

"I had in mind for you to let me hug you loosely and for you to put your cheek in close proximity with mine but without touching. Have I ever told you that my wife has the most extensive kitchen knife collection in Los Angeles? Have I also mentioned to you that her mother just gave her a brand new knife sharpener?" At the mention of June's knife collection, Little Matt crashed and burned like the Hindenburg at that navy base in New Jersey.

"Relax, junior, you're not my type. It just seems to me that if one is trying to fool someone, one should make one's deception realistic," said JoJo, with a smug smile. "Don't look now but Detweiller is driving away."

I looked up and saw that she was right. Detweiller was turning into an alley that led past the building and let out onto 6th Street. I hit the starter button with my foot, slammed the car into first gear and roared over to a position where I could see down the alley. I saw the Cadillac approaching 6th Street suddenly stop at the sidewalk and Detweiller reach over and open the passenger door. A young blonde woman appeared from behind the building, jumped into the front passenger seat and closed the door.

We followed the couple to a quiet street in Culver City. As we were driving I gave JoJo a crash course in how to tail someone in a vehicle. This time she listened intently and didn't make any snide comments. The Cadillac pulled to the curb near an apartment building. The couple got out and entered a first floor apartment and stayed inside for two hours. When they emerged I got some great pictures with my Leica of them kissing at the front door.

"What I don't understand," said JoJo later "is if this guy suspected he was being followed, why he decided to have that little play party with his girlfriend? I mean, why didn't he just lay low and stay out of trouble?"

"It's perfectly understandable to me. He was just thinking with his other head," I replied.

"Other head? What does that mean?"

"Never mind," I replied.

CHAPTER NINE

WEST HOLLYWOOD
LOS ANGELES
NOVEMBER 19, 1951
7:05 P.M.

The Havana nightclub was located on Sunset Boulevard near Larrabee. It was kind of a B-movie version of the much more glamorous (and well financed) Mocambo Club less than a mile away. On any given night at the Mocambo Club one might see Rita Hayworth, Humphrey Bogart, Ricardo Montalban and a plethora of other movie stars, accompanied by their Hollywood producer buddies and boyfriends, all enjoying themselves by getting blind drunk and then puking in the restroom sinks. At the Havana Club, by contrast one would see Hollywood short subject directors and producers, has-been actors and actresses from the silent and early talkies eras hoping against hope to run into somebody who could somehow get them back onto the silver screen, and actors from the new medium television, all rubbing shoulders with some of the most vicious gangsters in Los Angeles. They too amused themselves by getting blind drunk and then puking in the restroom sinks.

Both clubs had a Latin theme, but that's where the similarity ended. At the Mocambo, the owners had spent almost a million dollars on the décor and furnishings, including spotless white table cloths, silver plated flatware and crystal glassware. To further wow their clientele, the Mocambo displayed exotic wild birds in glass cages along one wall. At the Havana Club, by contrast, the table cloths were cheap cotton and dark brown so they could be reused by multiple customers throughout the evening. The knives, forks and spoons were of stainless steel, the glassware looked suspiciously like that sold on the bargain table at Woolworth's and the closest thing to a display of birds in the place was a mural on one wall depicting a line of storks all wearing little gaucho hats.

JoJo walked into the Havana club a little after seven, went directly to the bar and ordered a daiquiri. Five minutes later I limped in and bypassed the hat-check booth. The simple reason I didn't approach the pretty girl there was that I wasn't wearing a hat or coat. The weather that day had been in the high seventies and the temperature outside was still pleasantly mild. Once inside, I surveyed the place. It was only about a third full but it being Monday, and early in the evening, I didn't think too much of that. Up on a raised stage against the south wall of the building, three Latin looking men dressed as gauchos stood at tall, varnished wood drums, pounding out an incomprehensible melody. They were accompanied on the stage by three women, who also looked like they had their origins from someplace south of the border. They had on in long dresses with high hooded combs in their hair suggesting the ladies of colonial Mexico, as they shook polished gourds filled with pebbles in time with the drumbeat. Positioned around the room were six or seven tall, burly men in tuxedos, some with five o'clock shadows. I knew they were the club's bouncers, eager to short circuit any disturbance by ejecting the offenders out the back way into the alley.

I approached the nearest of these bouncers. "Do you work at this establishment?" I asked him in a businesslike voice. He looked at me with the fuddled gaze of an idiot.

"Yeah, what's it to you," he answered.

"I need to speak to the manager," I replied.

"Oh yeah, what about?"

"I need to ask him some questions about a young lady who works here. You see, my name is Watson and I am with the Internal Revenue Service."

The big bouncer was quiet for a few moments while all ten of his remaining brain cells had a conference about what I had just said. Maybe he had been dropped on a hard surface when he was a baby. But, then again, I knew that his job didn't require a lot of thinking. After a bit, the big man said, "Okay, follow me," and strode off across the floor, weaving between the tables. I limped after him trying to keep up with his fast pace.

As I passed one of the tables, a well-endowed woman in a low cut frock, obviously inebriated, leaned over to speak to the man sitting next to her and gave me a spectacular view of what the

Swiss Alps must look like in wintertime from an airplane high in the sky, with two little pink skiers waving to each other from opposite hillsides.

Little Matt: "Ow, wow, look at those. Can we stop a minute? Maybe you could pretend to tie your shoe so I could get a closer look."

The Brat: "C'mon, dumb ass, haven't you ever seen breasts before?"

I was so distracted that I almost ran into the back of the bouncer I was following. He had stopped at an unmarked door and was in the process of turning the doorknob to open it.

Following the bouncer through the door, I saw that the room I entered was fairly small, about the size of a normal kitchen, with a big desk cluttered with papers, dirty glasses and a huge overflowing ashtray taking up a most of the desktop, and with a window of one-way glass set into the wall behind it. The only occupants of the room were two men in tuxedos. One was of medium build with slicked back, pomaded hair, a dark complexion and thin mustache. He was sitting behind the desk smoking a cigarette. The other guy was much bigger and wider across the shoulders than the first. He was about my own age but had a full head of medium brown curly hair which made me a little jealous. His face displayed regular features but was a little too angular to be considered handsome. More concerning was the prominent bulge I spotted under his left armpit under the tailored cloth of his tuxedo. I knew he had a holstered handgun nestled there. That's okay, I thought, there are any number of legitimate reasons why a guy in his line of work guy might need to go around armed. Nevertheless, it was still disconcerting. When I entered the office, he was leaning against a wall with his arms folded and gazing at the floor like he was pondering some big problem.

"Boss," said the bouncer, "dis bird says he's from the gobermint. Says he needs to talk to you."

The man behind the desk snubbed out his cigarette in the big ashtray and looked up at me with a questioning expression. He signaled the bouncer to leave and he did. "What can we do for you?" he asked me.

"Yes," I said, as I pulled out my wallet, retrieved a business card and handed it to the seated man. "My name is Hiram P. Watson and I am from the Internal Revenue Service. I need to speak to one of your employees regarding a tax matter." The card was one from a collection of phony business cards I carried in a little box in the glove compartment of my Ford work car. The seated man glanced at the card then let it drop to the desk top.

"Okay Mr. Watson, which employee do you need to speak to?"

"I understand that the woman I need to talk to sometimes goes by the name of Rhonda Faye, but according to our records her real name is Daisy Carter," When I mentioned Rhonda's name, the head of the big guy leaning against the wall suddenly snapped up in surprise and his eyes bored into me. He pushed himself away from the wall and stepped slowly toward the desk.

"Eddie, take a walk, I'll handle this," said the big guy.

"Okay, Duke," answered Eddie, and left the room in a hurry. It was plain to see who was in charge here. The man just referred to as Duke sat down in the recently vacated chair behind the desk and fixed his eyes on me. He seemed wary and very alert and I wondered why.

"Okay, mister ah, what did you say your name was?"

"Watson, Hiram P. Watson," I replied.

"My name is Gallagher and I run this joint. So, Mr. Watson, I wasn't paying much attention to what you told my associate when you first walked in here, but I gather you want to speak to Rhonda Faye. Is that right?"

"That is correct, Mr. Gallagher. I'm with the Internal Revenue Service. Oh, yes, indeed, we are very interested in speaking to Miss Faye, although her real name is Miss Daisy Carter. Our records indicate that she has earned in excess of $3,650 in wages from this establishment through part of fiscal year 1949 and all of 1950 but has neglected to report this income by filing her form 1040 for these years. Together with fines and compound interest Miss Carter owes the government $412.69. I must speak to Miss Carter to warn her that if she doesn't pay what she owes before the 14th of next month, her fines and interest will double according to IRS schedule C-114. Of course, there is an appeal process. If Miss Carter files IRS Form G-345 in a timely manner, she possibly, and I emphasize possibly, may be granted a reduction in her fines. But then again there is also the possibility of an outright suspension of all the fines and accrued interest with a showing of compelling exigent circumstances under section 10-874 of the Internal Revenue Code. However, to take advantage of this law, Miss Carter will be required to appear in person at any IRS office. I must advise her that..."

"Hold on Mr. Watson," interrupted Duke Gallagher, holding up his hands with the palms out. "We don't know where Rhonda Faye is. She disappeared about a month ago. She didn't show up for work one evening and we haven't seen her since. So I'm afraid you came all the way down here for nothing. I'll tell you what. Why don't you stop at the bar on your way out for a drink on the house? Just tell the bartender that Duke said it was alright."

As I was being escorted out of the office by the bouncer, I was extremely worried about the wellbeing of Miss Daisy Carter. Duke Gallagher's reaction when I first spoke her name told the tale. If she was really okay and Duke and the boys were keeping her under wraps for some reason, they would probably let a man from the IRS speak to her.

Back out in the main lounge, I looked toward the stage. A sultry voiced singer in a full length, turquoise colored sequined dress was just completing the song "All My Love." Behind her on the stage was a chorus line of eight women in dark blue costumes with very short skirts who had their arms linked and were swaying in unison to the music. The song ended to polite applause. The singer stepped down from the stage and sat down at a table occupied by two well-heeled men. The chorus line exited stage right down a short flight of stairs and ducked into an unmarked door a few yards away. Stationed at the door was another muscle bound bouncer in a tuxedo. I headed to the bar.

JoJo was sitting on a stool at the bar and was now slumped over and draining the last drops from a long stemmed glass. As I slid onto the stool next to her she turned toward me with a lopsided grin on her face. The slump and the uncharacteristic grin told me that maybe my partner had consumed a wee bit too much alcohol.

"How many of those have you had?" I asked.

"Three. You know, I never cared much for drinking alcohol before, but these daiquiris are yummy. Jimmie the bartender here, he recommended them. They make me feel so relaxed."

"Are you sober enough to do something for me?"

"Well, that depends. If it entails taking off my clothes, then the answer is no, although you are kind of cute when you're not being a jerk. Anything non-sexual you want I'm up for," she replied slurring her speech just a wee bit.

"In about two minutes I want you to go out in the main lounge and create a ruckus on the side of the room away from the stage," I said.

"Ruckus? What do you mean by a ruckus?"

"A loud disturbance, use your imagination. It has to be boisterous enough to draw away all the bouncers from the stage area," I said.

I limped out of the bar and to a position against a wall about fifteen feet from the door I had seen the chorus line enter a few minutes ago. I watched JoJo leave the bar and stroll toward the main entrance. She appeared steady on her feet. Passing by a large bouncer, JoJo suddenly wheeled and slapped him across the mouth with all her might.

"YOU PINCHED ME! YOU MASHER! HOW DARE YOU?" she yelled in a shrill voice.

The slapped bouncer looked at her with a confused, shocked expression the way he would if she was a little green man who had just climbed out of a flying saucer in front of him and asked directions to the Grand Canyon. Every eye in the place except mine was pinned on JoJo.

"I DEMAND TO SPEAK TO THE MANAGER. THIS IS AN OUTRAGE!" yelled Jo-jo and tried to slap the bouncer again.

As I had hoped, every other bouncer in the place converged on the disturbance, including the one stationed outside the door I wanted to get in. Taking full advantage of the diversion I hurried to the door and quickly entered.

I was confronted by a long, narrow, brightly lit room. Along the right-hand wall were a line of dressing tables with mirrors and little stools. Eight young, attractive women were in various stages of undress sitting at the tables looking up at me.

"Excuse me, ladies," I said, holding up the snapshot of Daisy Carter. "I'm seeking the whereabouts of this woman. Her name is Daisy Carter."

"Who the hell are you," asked one of the women, as four others gathered around me to look at the picture. "I'm a private investigator. I was hired by Daisy Carter's boyfriend to find her. Has anybody seen her?" I asked. Most of the women shook their heads in a negative manner.

We were interrupted by a hatchet faced, no nonsense type woman in her fifties who entered the room through a door opposite to the one I had snuck in. "Who the hell are you?" she said. "Get the hell out of here!" Getting no response, she left through the same door she had entered a moment ago. I knew she was going to get a bouncer; therefore, I only had a minute at the most to speak to the showgirls.

"Are you sure nobody has seen her?" I asked. In response to my plea, a tall brunette wearing only her undies stood up from her stool, approached me, smiled and slipped something in my right coat pocket.

I heard the door open behind me and before I could turn to see who it was, I was grabbed from behind, pulled backward out of the dressing room and marched back to the club office. I say I marched but in actuality my feet were moving like I was walking but they never touched the ground the whole way. Unlike the last time I had been in the office less than fifteen minutes ago, I was searched, my wallet and gun were removed from me and I was plopped down into the same chair I had occupied before.

Duke Gallagher came breezing in and sat down across from me. One of the bouncers handed him my wallet and gun. At the sight of the big government model pistol, his eyes narrowed. After looking through my wallet he again looked up at me with a gaze that would freeze an Eskimo.

"So you're a gumshoe. I should have guessed. That suit you're wearing is far too expensive for a government bean counter. So tell me again why you're snooping around my club."

"I'm trying to locate a woman. Her name is Daisy Carter but she also has a stage name of Rhonda Faye," I answered.

"Who is your client?" asked Duke Gallagher.

"You know I can't tell you that," I replied.

"Do you want we should beat it out of him boss?" asked one of the bouncers.

Duke considered this for a moment then shook his head. "No Eddie, just give him a little taste of what will be in store for him if he ever comes snooping around here again." I was hauled to my feet and one of the goons slugged me hard in the solar plexus. It was a short punch, but delivered with speed and power with all his considerable weight behind it. It was painful. On a sliding scale of pain it was about midway between a toothache and passing a kidney stone. I doubled over and held my stomach until the hurting passed.

Duke slid my gun, clip of bullets and wallet across the table to me. "Okay, gumshoe," he said, menacingly "get your ass out of my club and don't come back." After stuffing my wallet and gun in my breast pocket, I was escorted out of the club, again without my feet touching the ground.

On my way to my car I retrieved the object that the half-naked showgirl had put in my pocket inside the club's dressing room. It turned out to be a book of matches from the Havana Club, but written on the inside was a message: "Call me tomorrow about ten, GR 2-4355." It was signed, "Charlene."

When I got to my car I saw JoJo leaning on the front fender. When she saw me she approached eagerly. "Did you see the look on that muscle bound idiot's face when I slapped him?" she asked with a wide smile. Her face was flushed and her eyes were sparkling. She really has beautiful eyes, I thought in a notion that seemed to come out of nowhere.

Captain Straight: "Whoa there Tex. Don't forget your wife's knife collection. And I'm sure the Viking Queen has them all honed razor sharp."

"I made such a fuss that the manager of the club gave me a hundred dollars just to go away and leave them alone," JoJo said. And then in almost a little girl's voice she asked. "Did I do well?"

"Yes, JoJo, you did very well. I'll make a detective of you yet."

CHAPTER TEN

ARLINGTON HEIGHTS
LOS ANGELES
NOVEMBER 19, 1951
9:45 P.M.

JoJo and I had been sitting in my car outside Daisy Carter's apartment building for going on two hours. Before that I had treated her to a chili burger for dinner at one of my favorite places to eat, Tommy's Hamburgers at Beverly and Rampart. The food as well as the passing time had erased JoJo's alcohol induced good humor. Now the combative façade she showed to the world was back up and on full display. She was fidgeting on the seat beside me and complaining non-stop.

"How long do we have to sit here?" she whined. "It's been twenty minutes since the lights went off in that old geezer Hilton's apartment?"

"It takes normal people from ten to thirty minutes to fall asleep, and sometimes longer if you're old like Mr. Hilton. And how do we know what's really going on in that apartment? Mrs.

Hilton might be a geriatric nymphomaniac and could be draining the last of the vital fluids out of the old guy as we speak. No, we have to wait for a full thirty minutes after the lights go out," I replied as I fired up another Lucky Strike cigarette and blew the smoke toward the windshield. JoJo's response was the same as with the last five cigarettes I had smoked. She cranked down the passenger window and stuck her head partway out to escape the smoke. But after a while, because the night air had turned decidedly chilly, she wound it back up again with an exasperated expression.

"How many of those filthy things do you smoke in a day? Aren't you worried about your health?"

"I don't know. I don't keep count. The doctor who examined me at my last physical told me to keep on smoking. He said the relaxation effect of smoking cigarettes far outweighs any harmful physical drawbacks. And he was smoking a Camel himself as he said that."

"Well that's just dandy. To get this relaxation effect you impose your foul smoke on others, but being a man you're oblivious to the harm your conduct inflicts on others. My new outfit will smell like an ashtray for a week," said Jo-jo.

"Well, you could always quit your job and go sit on a hilltop somewhere, breathe the pure air and complain to the world about how unfair life has been to you."

"Never," replied Jo-jo vehemently.

At five minutes to ten I glanced at the façade of the apartment building. Almost all the windows were dark. I figured that it was now or never to search Daisy Carter's apartment. "Let's go," I told JoJo, handed her a small flashlight identical to the one I had in my jacket pocket and opened the driver's side door.

As we approached the front entrance to the building I hoped that my bootleg key would fit in the lock. Making a key from an impression in clay was an art not a science. The chances that the one I held in my hand now wouldn't work were frighteningly high. I put the key into the outside lock. It was standard procedure for apartment owners in Los Angeles to issue one key to their tenants that fit the main entrance as well as their apartment doors. Once inserted, I turned the key gently to the left and was relieved when there was no resistance to my action. The bolt slid smoothly back and the door opened.

The vestibule was a somewhat dimly lit rectangular room about six or seven feet wide and ten or so feet long. A panel containing brass mailboxes occupied the left wall. Each individual mailbox had a small glass window so that the tenant could tell at a glance if they had any mail. I saw the gleam of white in Daisy's mailbox, indicating that she had at least one piece of mail. Two hallways led off from the vestibule to the right and left to access the doors to the apartments on the first floor. Facing us at the end of the room was a broad stairway leading to the upper floors.

Treading lightly so as not to make any noise and arouse a curious tenant, we crept up the stairs to the second floor and down the hall to Daisy's apartment door. Once again my illegal key functioned flawlessly. Once inside JoJo and I stood still for a few moments in the dark listening but heard nothing. I took my flashlight from my pocket and snapped it on but was careful to restrict the beam emitting from it with my fingers. I saw a folded sheet of paper lying on the floor just inside the door. Apparently someone had shoved it under the door. I picked it up and examined it. The paper was a note from Carlo, pleading with Daisy to please contact him. Even though he had hired me, the poor guy was still looking on his own. He must have been here within the last day or so because the note hadn't been here when Hilton showed JoJo and me the apartment. The next thing I did was to walk around the apartment pulling down all the window shades. Once that was accomplished I turned on a small lamp on an end table beside the sofa, shut off my flashlight and put it back in my pocket.

The apartment was laid out with the door to the bedroom directly across the living room and opposite the front door. The kitchenette was in an alcove to the left with a small two person vinyl table fronting it. The bathroom was accessed using a door to the right.

"I'm going to start searching in the bathroom," I whispered to JoJo. "When I come out I want you to search the bathroom and then follow me around and search the same places I do. It's always helpful to have more than one pair of eyes while casing a place. I could miss something important and not even know it."

"Okay Mr. boss man, I need to know one thing," JoJo whispered back.

"What's that?"

"What am I searching for?" she asked in an exasperated whisper.

"Anything that doesn't fit its surroundings and that you think seems out of place. Also be on the lookout for photographs, letters, papers that she has tried to hide because that means she doesn't want anyone to see them."

I came up empty in the bathroom except for a lunch sized brown paper bag stashed in the cabinet under the sink. Inside were about twenty-five condoms, each individually wrapped in foil and unused.

Captain Straight: "It looks like Daisy and Carlo are further along in their relationship than he lets on, or Miss Carter has other boyfriends that she's intimate with. Enough to keep a year's supply of condoms on hand."

There were other possibilities, but I put them out of my mind for the time being and moved on to the bedroom. At first glance the bedroom was like a lot of single women's bedrooms in the country, all frilly, ruffled and knicknacky and included stuffed animals and other childhood mementos. But very few of those other bedrooms would be as neat and tidy as this one. Everything in the room right down to the combs and brushes on the dressing table were laid out with surgical precision. It appeared that Miss Daisy Carter was a neat freak. I took my time and searched slowly and carefully but came up empty. As I walked through the door into the living room, I glanced behind me and saw JoJo enter the bedroom, dutifully doing what I had instructed her to do.

As I was searching through the cans of food in the kitchenette, (sometimes people keep money or secret things in special deliberately mislabeled food containers), I was feeling a little frustrated. The only thing helpful I had found was Daisy's mailbox key. I had discovered it hanging on a nail in the kitchenette wall. Jo-jo walked out of the door of the bedroom and approached me. She was carrying an object that looked like a book in her hands.

"I found this scotch taped to the underside of the dressing table top" she said, and handed the object to me beaming like a schoolgirl showing her teacher that she had found Singapore on a world map.

The object was a small bound book. It was about six by eight inches in size and an inch thick. It was covered in cheap red imitation leather and looked similar to the variety of small diaries and notebooks on sale at Woolworth's five-and–dime for less than fifty cents. JoJo stood at my side and watched as I opened the book to the first page and noticed a smaller maroon colored folder tucked into a pocket attached to the inside of the front cover. Extracting the folder from the pocket, I saw that it was a bankbook issued by the Farmers & Merchant's Bank for an account in the name of Daisy Ann Carter. I flipped through the small pages and saw a long list of deposits going back to early 1950. The last line showed that the account had $6,782.76 in it. This was a lot of money for a chorus girl supposedly making sixty dollars a week to possess. The average wage for a working man in the current economy was a dollar an hour. I put the bankbook in my jacket pocket and concentrated on the red book.

"JACK B." was handwritten in capital letters across the top of the first page of the book. Written underneath the name was an address: 5165 Wilshire Blvd. and a phone number: WI 56475. "MS on desktop" and "only weekdays from 12 to 1" was written on the next line. The next entries on the page were a series of dates, followed by a dollar amount. The earliest dates had $50 written beside them. But the later ones had amounts ranging from $80 to $100 jotted in next to them with some that had a plus sign after the amount and a further amount written down, usually $20.

At the very bottom of the page was written: "Nice guy, quick, not too rough."

I flipped through the pages of the book. Twenty-five pages of the book had writing on them in Daisy's hand. They all appeared to follow a similar pattern. In the top left hand corner of the first page a john's name was written, but only a first name followed by the first initial of his last name. To the right of the name on the top line were cryptic abbreviations." Underneath the name on the second line was a phone number and beside that, notations on the time of day or week. The third line contained comments like

"Nice guy not too rough," or "Likes his back rubbed." The rest of the page listed a series of dates and beside each was a dollar amount. After some of the dollar amounts Daisy had written a plus sign and another dollar amount, usually $20, probably indicating a tip.

"Well, JoJo," I said, "now we know how Daisy Carter is able to afford such nice furniture and has over six grand in the bank. It appears that she is a high class call girl and this is her john book."

"By call girl, do you mean prostitute? And what the hell is a john book?"

"I'm afraid so. A john book is a record kept by a prostitute mainly so she can remember her client's sexual preferences for their next encounter. This one though is a lot more detailed than most."

JoJo took the book from my hand and turned the pages. "What do these abbreviations mean?" she asked, pointing out several pages where "BJ," "MS," and "DS" and the like were written.

"Well, "BJ" means "Blow Job." "MS" means "missionary sex" and "DS" means "doggie style." Do you want me to go on?" I asked, trying not to smile at her anticipated reaction.

"That's disgusting," replied JoJo, made a face and pushed the book away. For my part I started thinking of ways to break this news to Carlo the mountain-and-a-half without ending up at the bottom of Santa Monica Bay twisted into a pretzel shape.

We both froze as we detected the sound of footsteps out in the hall and then the sound of a key being inserted in the lock. I slipped the red book into my jacket pocket and turned to face the door.

The apartment door swung open to reveal a tall, thin soldier in uniform. He was in his early twenties with dark hair cut short under his barracks cap. Right now his regular, handsome features were screwed up into an angry scowl and his fingers were balled into fists.

"Who the hell are you and what are you doing in my sister's apartment?" he snarled.

"Now hold on there, soldier, this is not what you think. We're private detectives," I said, while showing him my investigator identification and handing him a business card. "We were hired by your sister's boyfriend, a big guy named Carlo, to find her. We were just looking for some clue that would point to her whereabouts."

"Is Carlo the wrestler?" asked the soldier.

"Yes, he wrestles under the name of 'Ivan, the Red Menace.'"

"Yeah, Daisy told me about the wrestler. She said she loved the guy. Well I guess you people are okay. I'd like to help you in any way I can to find Daisy. I haven't seen her in a month and I've been worried sick. Our parents are dead and other than an aunt who raised us, we have no other relatives so she's the only person I have left in the world."

"So you have no idea where Daisy Carter is." I asked.

"No. Like I said, she has been gone for a month, October 21st to be exact. We had plans to go out to dinner that night, but when I got here she was gone. Ever since then I come by her apartment whenever I can hoping she has shown up but so far she hasn't. That's how I caught you. I swung by the apartment on the way back to my billet at Fort MacArthur and saw the cracks of light around the window shades and knew that somebody was in the apartment. I thought it was Daisy and got all excited," said the soldier, looking at the floor sadly. JoJo reached out a hand and put it on the soldier's arm to comfort him. Her eyes were about to tear up, I was sure of it.

"By the way, I'm Matt Cole and this is JoJo Marx. I didn't catch your name."

"It's Sam, Sam Carter, private, United States Army. I got back from Korea in September and since I only have a few months left on my enlistment, the army sent me to Fort MacArthur to wait out the time. I don't have any duties except attending morning formations so I have time to help you find my sister. By the way, did you find anything in your search of the apartment?"

"Only this," I replied and handed him his sister's maroon bankbook. Sam opened the little book.

"Holy cow! How did my sister get so much money? Something is fishy here."

The Brat: "It's fishy all right, ten day old tuna fishy."

"So Sam, is there a number where we can contact you and keep you apprised on the developments of the case?" I asked.

"Sure, there's a telephone in the company office. They should be able to get ahold of me if I'm on the base. If you give me a pencil and something to write on, I'll give it to you," Sam said. But then I realized that Sam was no longer talking to me but to Jojo. He was staring at her like a lovesick calf and starting to pant. I glanced over at JoJo. She was gazing back at him like he was Cary Grant and Gary Cooper rolled into one. Her face was flushed, her breathing was rapid and a vein at the base of her throat was throbbing noticeably through the skin. I had the feeling that if I wasn't there, piles of clothing would be littering the floor within twenty minutes.

The Brat: "Isn't it romantic? A true case of lust at first sight that doesn't happen very often."

Captain Straight: "Not so unusual, they're both young healthy mammals of prime mating age. You see it every day in the monkey cage at the zoo."

After Sam had jotted down a phone number on the back of another of my business cards I tucked it safely away in my wallet. "So, Sam," I said to him, "go on back to the base. We will get hold of you if there are any developments in the case or we need your assistance for any reason."

Sam left the apartment and JoJo stared to follow him but I stopped her with a hand on her arm. She turned to me with a questioning look. "Let him get out of the area. I want to examine those letters in Daisy's mailbox I saw on the way in and I don't want Sam to be here when I do. They might contain information we don't want anybody but us to see." JoJo nodded.

We waited a whole five minutes then locked the apartment door and went downstairs to the lobby. I put the key in the mailbox lock and retrieved two letters from the box, both addressed to Daisy Carter. I looked at the outside of the envelopes in the dim light of the lobby. One appeared to be a phone bill from Ma Bell. The other was from a place called "Saint Gertrude's Home for Girls," at a Santa Barbara address. I stuffed the two envelopes in my jacket pocket.

Back in the car I turned to my young partner. "JoJo," I said, pompously, "number one on the list of no-nos for a private detective is to get emotionally involved with someone connected to a case you're working on."

'What the hell do you mean?" she blurted, sat back in the car seat, folded her arms and gave me an angry look.

"I saw the way you were looking at Sam back in that apartment. I was waiting for your tongue to shoot out and slurp him up like an African tree frog taking down a tsetse fly."

CHAPTER ELEVEN

WILSHIRE DISTRICT
LOS ANGELES
NOVEMBER 20, 1951
9:50 A.M.

T he first thing I did when I entered my private office was to take off my suit jacket and brush off the droplets of water that clung to it before hanging it on my bentwood coat rack. It was raining buckets outside. My morning commute had been a snarled mess. It had taken me a whole twenty-minutes to drive to the office instead of the usual ten. Next, I got my gun from the bottom drawer of my desk and slipped it into my waistband at the back, retrieved from my hip pocket the red leatherette covered john book and the matchbook given to me by Charlene at the Havana Club and sat down. Then I remembered the two letters I had snagged from Daisy's mailbox. I stood up again and pulled the letters from my coat pocket and then sat down again.

JoJo came sauntering in and sat down across the desk from me with her arms folded. "Sam Carter says he remembers something else," she said. "He said he noticed some unusually bad bruises on his sister's arms a few weeks ago. When he asked her about them, she was very evasive in her answer, saying she fell down in a parking lot."

"And how would you know about this new revelation by Sam Carter?" I asked.

"He called while I was waiting the usual hour for you to show up for work. Since you weren't here, I took the call,' she replied belligerently.

"Did he say anything else? Where exactly were the bruises? Did they look like they had been caused by a man's hands squeezing them?"

"I don't know. Sam said he had to go see the first sergeant or somebody like that and couldn't talk any more. I'll ask him about it when I see him and get further information. We have a date on Friday Night."

"Weren't you listening when I gave my pompous little speech about not getting involved with principles in cases you investigate?" I asked, frowning like Ellen O'Hara did at that dastardly overseer Wilkinson.

"First off, Sam is not a principal in the case, He's just related to a principal. And second, you don't get to tell me where I go or who I see on my own time," replied JoJo, climbing up on an extremely high horse.

"You're always after me to fire you. And I will if you pull something like this little stunt again," I said, bluntly. JoJo frowned and looked back at me with a stubborn set to her jaw.

The Brat: "You're a funny one to say something like that. Remember Elaine Torgelson? As I recall she was a principal in a case and you screwed her on every horizontal surface of her house, including on top of her washing machine. I think you're being a tad hypocritical."

"Alright," I said, feeling suitably chastened, "we'll talk about this later."

Using the letter opener on my desk I slit open the envelope containing the letter to Daisy from Santa Barbara. I unfolded the paper inside and discovered that it was a quarterly bill for room and board for someone named Amelia Carter from an entity called the Saint Gertrude Home for Girls. The amount of the bill was for $176.00. Opening the phone bill in a similar manner, I saw that during the month of October, Daisy had made sixteen message unit calls to various prefixes around Los Angeles, but only three long distance calls. All of them were to a Santa Barbara exchange and were all about the same duration- ten minutes, sometimes a little more, sometimes a little less.

Putting the letters back down on my desk, I picked up the receiver of my private phone and dialed the number Charlene had written in the inside of the matchbook she had slipped in my pocket the night before. The phone rang five times at the other end and then an elderly female voice answered. "Ma Kincaid's Rooming House. Ma speaking."

"Yes, I need to speak to Charlene," I said.

"Just a minute, I'll go get her." I waited, twiddling my thumbs for about five minutes. Then a much younger sounding female voice came on the line. "This is Charlene."

"Yeah, this is Matthew Cole. I'm a private investigator. Last night at the Havana Club you gave me a matchbook with your phone number written inside, I presume you have some information about the whereabouts of Daisy Carter."

"No, I have no idea where Daisy is. There are just some things that you need to know because it's not right the way the girls at the club are treated. I've danced there about two months. When I first got there I met Daisy and we were both Midwestern girls who had come out to California to try to make it in movies so we hit it off right away. She was a good kid but always seemed so sad and I wondered why. But then I found out. The manager of the place, Duke Gallagher, started to pressure me to go out and sleep with wealthy customers of the club for money and then give him a cut afterward. I told him I wasn't a whore and he backed off for a while, but lately he's been at me again to do it. He even roughed me up a little bit a few nights ago. Daisy finally broke down and told me that she was involved in the whoring when I saw some bad bruises on her back one night. She also said that most of the other girls that work at the Havana Club are doing it too. She said that she hadn't wanted to do it but Duke had threatened her into doing it. She was a young gal all alone in the world except for a brother but he was off in Korea. It started off as one guy and he was young and handsome and before she knew it there were many more."

"When is the last time you saw Daisy Carter?" I asked.

"Let me see, it was about a month ago on a Saturday night. It had to have been on October twentieth. I remember the date because it was the same day I had a doctor's appointment to have a boil lanced on my bottom. Daisy said she had a date that night with a guy who treated her extra bad and she was a little scared to go. Duke had refused her requests to drop the guy, threatening her in the process. She said she had another client on a regular basis who was too rough with her but not like the guy she was seeing that night. Listen, I hope you keep all this under your hat. If it got out that I told you all this stuff I could be in serious trouble. Duke might beat me to death."

"You have no worries on that score. I won't tell anyone, I promise. But my advice to you Charlene is to pack your bags and catch the first bus going east and go back home."

"You're probably right. I'll think about it."

'Oh, by the way, did Daisy ever mention that she had a kid in a girl's home in Santa Barbara?" I asked thinking about the letter on my desk top in front of me. There was silence on the line for quite a while and then Charlene answered, but she sounded very reluctant.

"I promised Daisy that I wouldn't tell anyone about that. But now that she's missing and nobody knows what happened to her, maybe I should tell you. I mean, it's nothing to be really ashamed of I guess. Yeah, Daisy has a kid, a little girl. She told me one night when we were both down in the dumps that when she first came to California she fell in with a guy and got pregnant and the guy promptly deserted her. She planned to have the baby in a home for unwed girls and then put it up for adoption. But Daisy told me that when she delivered the baby and saw her for the first time she fell so in love with the little thing that she couldn't give her up. If you want my opinion, I think Daisy first started whoring for Duke just to get enough money to take care of that little girl."

After I hung up the phone I filled in JoJo on what Charlene had said. She was outraged.

"I can't believe that this can happen in the United States of America in 1951. We should do something. Maybe we could call the police and blow the whistle on this whole thing," she said.

"It's become a lot more complicated than that. I knew from the start that the Manila Club was a hangout for Chicago gangsters affiliated with Jack Dragna. Now I have a possible reason for that. Daisy may have been sucked in to one of Jack Dragna's prostitution rackets being run out of the club. If that is so, we could call the cops all day and not get any action. A third of the L.A. cops are on Dragna's payroll. This revelation also means that the danger level of this case has just risen through the roof.

I'm gonna talk to Caroline Adderley about getting your training reassigned to another detective. This one could get us both killed."

"Nonsense, you'll do no such thing. I'm a big girl. If I should get hurt or killed it will be nobody's fault but my own. Please don't take me off this case. I'm really hooked. I love doing this." she said with a plaintive tone to her voice.

"Alright, let me think about it for a while," I responded.

I took a yellow legal pad from a shelf behind my desk, swung around and opened Daisy's john book. As quickly as I could write, I listed the phone number for each of Daisy's clients copied from the pages of the red book in a column down the left hand side of the pad. When I was finished, I handed the tablet to JoJo.

"Go into the bullpen and use the reverse directory to find out who these numbers belong to," I told her.

'What's a reverse directory?"

"You know how the phone book lists people in the city in alphabetical order with their phone numbers to the right of the name?" I asked and JoJo nodded her head that she understood. "Well the reverse directory lists phone numbers in numerical sequence and who they belong to after. The company that sells them claims that every phone number in Los Angeles is in there, but they aren't. Anyway, you can't miss it; it's a big ass book about two foot square and three inches thick. And be gentle with it. The damn things cost me over a hundred bucks a copy." JoJo nodded, and left my office.

When she was gone I picked up the red john book, and read carefully through the twenty-five pages that had entries on them for the first time. When I finished I had plenty of food for thought.

Most of Daisy's johns had sexual preferences that were within the range of normal for a call girl to fulfill. Three pages had the notation "RS" written after the name. I surmised that this abbreviation stood for rough sex. This was still normal. Very few men were gentle with prostitutes. But two of the johns were different. On two pages of her john book, Daisy had taken a red pencil and drawn a crude skull and crossbones symbol, indicating that these guys described on these pages were poison. One of these pages with the danger symbol was labeled with the name "Alistair C." and "S&M" was listed as a preference, indicating that the guy was a sado-masochist. On the other page with a danger symbol, "Mike C." was written at the top, but there was no preference listed. Instead there was a cryptic note that read: "mean and chokes." The presence of the poison symbols, written by Daisy's own hand, catapulted these two johns to the top of the list of suspects who might have done her harm and might be responsible for her disappearance.

The next thing I did was look at dates. Daisy had listed the date of every tryst. She made it easy for me to identify the johns she had serviced in the week leading up to her disappearance. I was disappointed. I had hoped I would find a pattern of some sort or something unusual, but there wasn't anything. Daisy went on "dates" with five different men listed in the john book. I tried going back another week but it was the same, this time six different men.

Then something caught my eye. Daisy's date for the two Friday nights was the same guy, Alistair C. I turned to his page in the john book and nodded in satisfaction. Except for a missed week here and there, every Friday night going back almost eight months, Daisy and Alistair C. had a date. More ominously, Alistair C. was one of the guys she had labeled with the red skull and crossbones.

As I was concentrating on the john book, Jojo came back into the room carrying the legal pad. She plopped it down in front of me.

"Out of the twenty-five phone numbers, sixteen were listed. I wrote down the name listed as the owner after the number. Half of them are just the names of companies. The rest I couldn't get. The directory noted that they are unlisted numbers," said JoJo. She had a yellow pencil tucked over her right ear and she looked as happy as a girl on the way to her senior prom.

I wasn't surprised about the numbers. It stood to reason that men who could afford Daisy's large fee for services would be businessmen, with private lines in their offices. It shouldn't be too hard to find the names of the johns if I needed to by calling their companies and using a little Matt Cole bullshit. The numbers for the two johns Daisy was afraid of were unlisted.

"What about the unlisted numbers? asked JoJo.

"I can get those too, but it will be a little harder. I have a contact inside the phone company," I answered. I flipped through my rolodex, retrieved a number and dialed it on my private line.
When the PBX operator came on the line, I asked for Myron Ham.

"This is Myron Ham. How may I assist you?"

"Myron, old buddy, this is Matt Cole. I have some unlisted numbers and I need to know who they belong to."

"Why Matt Cole, I haven't heard from you in some time. I thought you must have retired. I read somewhere that you inherited a boatload of money. You said numbers. How many numbers are we talking about?"

"Ten."

"Can you drop a list of the numbers by my office or do you want to mail it to me?"

"No, I'll come by your office in about an hour. Is the price still the same? Ten bucks a number?"

"Still the same. I'll see you in an hour," said Myron, and hung up.

"I'm beginning to think that everyone in Los Angeles is corrupt except me. The phone company too?" said JoJo in amazement.

"Yep, Ma Bell is a crusty old slut," I replied. "Here, make yourself useful. Write out a list of the unlisted numbers we want to find out about on a clean sheet of paper from the pad. Make sure you write legibly. I don't want to have to pay extra money because you're sloppy." JoJo made a face at me.

CHAPTER TWELVE

WILSHIRE DISTRICT
LOS ANGELES
NOVEMBER 20, 1951
11:00 A.M.

A s I was backing my old Ford out of its parking place in front of my office, a long black Cadillac pulled up and stopped blocking me in. I waited a moment for it to move; then after telling JoJo to sit tight in the passenger seat, I got out to find out what the Cadillac occupants wanted. I kept my right hand a little way behind my back close to my gun in case I had to defend myself.

As I neared the back of my car, the back door of the Cadillac opened and a well-built man of about thirty and wearing a good suit stepped out and looked me in the eye. From the moment he appeared I had no doubt what he was an L.A. gangster. The only question was what faction he was with, Cohen's or Dragna's.

"Matthew Cole, Mr. Stompanato would like a word with you," said the gangster in a level voice.

Now every person in Los Angeles in a line of work that necessitated him nibbling around the fringes of the gang underworld knew that name and that included me. The gangster could only be referring to John "Johnny Stomp" Stompanato, lieutenant to Mickey Cohen, chief of the L.A. rackets. I peered into the car and saw "Johnny Stomp" himself sitting on the back seat. His handsome Italian face wore a wide smile.

"Step inta the car for a moment, will ya? We got some things to discuss," called Stompanato.

I could see that I was trapped. Short of pulling my gun and initiating a shootout, there was no way I was going to avoid getting in that car. So I went with the flow and sat down beside the mob boss with him on my left.

"Where to boss?" asked the driver, another hood similar to the first one.

"Just drive around the block a coupla times, Eddie. This won't take long," replied Stompanato. I didn't know if that was good news or bad news for me. I would just have to wait and see.

Once the big Caddie was moving, "Johnny Stomp" lit a cigarette with a gold lighter and turned his face toward me.

"We been hearin a rumor bouncing round town in the last few days. This rumor says that because of your past associations with our organization, you are an in to Mickey Cohen for anybody in the Dragna organization thinkin bout jumpin ship.

Now Mickey and I are stumped as to how this could be, seein as we made no such arrangement with you. You have any idea how that rumor got started?"

"Beats the hell out of me," I lied. "I mean, look at it from my side. Why would I willingly insert myself between two warring gang factions? I could be bumped off by either side. I'm not that stupid."

"Mickey and I talked it over and we agree with ya. It would be stupid on your side. So we believe ya. But we decided that we're gonna take advantage of the situation. If any of Dragna's boys get ahold of ya wantin ta switch sides we want ya to call us right away," said the mob boss and handed me a slip of paper with a phone number written on it. "If I was you I'd keep a sharp lookout for Dragna's people from now on. He's not gonna be real happy with you when he hears them rumors," said Stompanato, as I was stepping out of his car back in front of my office.

The Brat: "And that ladies and gentlemen, is what a major backfire looks like. Chief Parker's little baited trap has wound up catching the family dog instead of that pesky gopher. The captain was right about this crazy idea from the beginning."

Captain Straight: "Johnny Stomp is right about Dragna being upset you know. You're in a real pickle."

JoJo got out of the Ford and joined me at the rear of the vehicle as I watched the big Cadillac drive away.

"What was that all about? Who were those people?" she asked with her arms folded.

"Just some guys I know. We get together on weekends to play softball in MacArthur Park."

"Those men didn't look like the kind of people who play softball for recreation except in prison. They looked like gangsters. Something is going on here that you're not telling me about," she said.

"We need to go back inside. I need to make an urgent phone call," I said and headed back inside my office with JoJo on my heels. Once inside I picked up the receiver of my private line and dialed the number in city hall that Lieutenant Miller had given me after my meeting with Chief Parker. The call was answered after two rings.

"Chief's office, Sergeant Brown speaking."

"I need to speak with Lieutenant Miller. My name is Matt Cole and it's urgent," I said into the mouthpiece.

"He just stepped down the hall for a minute. Give me a number where you can be reached and I'll have him call you as soon as he gets back," replied the sergeant. I gave him the number of my private line and hung up the phone.

JoJo, who was sitting across the desk from me, looking pissed off, chimed in: "Tell me what's going on here. I 'm supposed to be your partner. I have a right to know."

I thought about it for a few moments and then decided to level with her. I told her about my meeting with Chief Parker and what I had agreed to do for him. As I told the story, the expression on JoJo's face went from anger to amazement and finally to something like admiration.

"So, JoJo, remember earlier when I told you that working with me had suddenly become too dangerous. Well, as of now, acting as my partner has just become condition red dangerous. I'm going to have to insist that you be reassigned to another detective for your training. I might not be alive very much longer and I don't want to get you killed as an unfortunate side effect."

She stood defiantly and put her hands on her hips. "Now isn't that just like a man? You all feel you have to protect the frail little female from harm like some kind of white knight or something. I can take care of myself. Every evening since you hired me, instead of going home, I've been going to the pistol range and practicing with my gun. I've gotten pretty good with it too. You can't handle this mess you've gotten yourself into alone. You need somebody to help keep you alive in case those bastards try to sneak up on you from behind while you're not looking. Anyway, I don't care what you say. I'm staying whether you like it or not. So just shut the hell up about reassigning me, okay?"

Captain Straight: "She's got guts, I'll give that to her."

The Brat: "You better hang on to this one. She's a keeper."

"Okay, Detective Marx, we'll still be partners, but don't ever say I didn't warn you," I replied, just before the phone rang.

"What's wrong?" asked Lieutenant Miller, his voice sounding like he was speaking in a tunnel. I quickly told the cop about my meeting with John "Johnny Stomp' Stompanato, and we discussed the implications. "I thought you were just going to speak a few words in the ear of some people close to that bent captain. I didn't know you were going to broadcast my affiliation with the Cohen mob over fifty-thousand watt KFI right between the sports scores and the commercial for Carter's Little Liver Pills," I said, more than a little annoyed. And I had more to say. "I'm concerned about my safety, but I'm more concerned about my wife and baby at home. I'm going to need round the clock security for them. You got me into this, now you're going to have to protect my family."

"Take it easy," replied Miller trying to sooth me. "The chief has a special squad of some of the toughest, meanest bastards I've ever seen and this will be right up their alley. Rest assured, your wife and child will be as safe as they would be in a vault in the Bank of England. The best part is your wife will never know that they're around."

§

Jojo and I arrived at the Pacific Telephone and Telegraph office in the 700 block of South Olive Street at around two in the afternoon. Five minutes later I was handing the list of unlisted phone numbers to Myron Ham. He was a little prissy guy with glasses. He looked like a high school principal. Actually, Myron was an okay guy. He just had this little gambling problem that necessitated him earning extra money now and then. JoJo and I sat down in the small reception area to wait. In about a half hour, Myron called us back to his cramped little office and handed me a white legal size envelope. I handed him a c-note with a flourish. With everyone in the room smiling in satisfaction, JoJo and I walked out to my Ford and were seated in the front seat before I opened the envelope.

I unfolded the page containing the names and addresses connected to the unlisted numbers and spread it out on my knee. I then took out the red john book. The guy I was most interested in was a john labeled "Al C." on one of the two pages Daisy had decorated with a skull and crossbones symbol. The guy apparently was her regular Saturday night date and this, coupled with the fact that according to Charlene Daisy had disappeared on a Saturday night made the guy a prime suspect. I compared the two references and got a bit of a shock. I learned the identity of Al and that the telephone that rang when someone dialed the phone number in the john book was located in a mansion on Fairing Road in Holmby hills, one of the poshest areas in Los Angeles. Al's identity complicated the hell out of my investigation. "Shit," I said.

"What's wrong?" asked JoJo.
"The lessee of the phone connected to that number is Alistair Corning the movie actor."

'I don't recognize the name but then again I don't go to a lot of movies." replied JoJo.

"He's an English actor that moved to Hollywood during the war years and stayed. The guy is a tall, slim and distinguished looking mustachioed man in his late thirties with a baritone voice. During his career at Mammoth Studios, he's appeared in a bunch of pictures and seems to be well liked by critics and audiences. He could probably get some lead roles, but so far he has confined himself to supporting roles as the third person in a love triangle, the stalwart older brother, best friend of the star, or an authority figure. A few years back he appeared as a cavalry colonel in a western, I forget the name. There was talk around Hollywood that he would be nominated for a best supporting actor Oscar, but he wasn't. What I don't understand is why a guy like this would be involved with a prostitute. I mean he's handsome and rich; those homes in Holmby Hills go for a hundred and fifty thousand bucks or sometimes more. And being in movies, with the money and the house, the guy must have women crawling all over him," I told her.

"I suggest we just walk up to this Alistair Corning and ask him about Daisy,"

"That's easier said than done. Guys like him have several layers of people separating them from the great unwashed underlings in the general public. He'll have a personal bodyguard, maybe more than one and there will surely be additional security people guarding the perimeter of his home. Their job is to guarantee that no one gets near him without his consent. The next level of people keeping him away from the likes of you and me are his agent, his publicist and his studio handlers. Actors can often be incredible bigmouths and drunks and say offensive things that might affect box office receipts. For this reason they are kept on a tight leash. The third level of security is the police. If you think the estates in Holmby Hills don't get a damn sight more patrol time than the houses of us peons in the low rent districts, you're mistaken. We might be okay if we drive my Cadillac, but in this old heap we wouldn't get three blocks into the neighborhood before being stopped by a patrol car. I guess we could dress up as a maid and butler and pretend we are returning to an estate from an outing at the beach on our day off. But that wouldn't work. I don't think I could persuade you in a hundred years to put on one of those short little maid's uniforms and call yourself "Fifi."

"So what are we going to do?" asked JoJo, ignoring my attempt at humor.

"I don't know," I replied and fired up another Lucky Strike, which prompted JoJo to roll down her window and fan the smoke away from her face with her hand.

CHAPTER THIRTEEN

HOLLYWOOD
LOS ANGELES
NOVEMBER 21, 1951
1:02 P.M.

I pulled up behind a tan Buick at the Mammoth Studios gate on Melrose. I was driving my new Cadillac and wearing my best suit. I watched the guard holding a clipboard deal with the occupant of the Buick. The guard was a middle aged guy with a decidedly no nonsense attitude who didn't appear to smile much, if ever.

The Brat: "I bet this asshole kicks his dog twice when he comes home from work, just to keep the soles of his shoes limber."

A few minutes later the guard walked a few steps to a stanchion beside the driveway and pushed a button. The double gates on the phony mission revival style façade swung open majestically and the car ahead of me drove through. The guard gave me a scowl and motioned me forward. I took the space just vacated by the Buick, stopped and cranked down my window.

"What can I do for you bub?" asked the guard in a brash voice perfectly in character with his observed demeanor.

"Yeah, I have an appointment with a guy named Oliver P. Tompkins," I said levelly. "I think he said that he was twenty-third deputy assistant to the second deputy of the vice president in charge of public relations."

"Very funny," said the guard, but his face betrayed the fact that he didn't think it was funny at all. "And who might you be bub?"

"I'm Matthew Cole. I'm a private investigator."

The guard consulted a list attached to the clipboard. "Alright," he said, "you drive straight ahead past three sound stages. You'll see an office building on your right. Park in the lot in front and go inside and speak to the receptionist. She will direct you further." The grouchy guard stepped back, pushed his button and the gates to Paramount Studios swung open majestically.

§

Sitting in my Ford with JoJo outside the phone company headquarters the day before; I had been at a loss as to how to proceed with the investigation. I finally fired up the car and headed back to the office.

"Why not just follow Corning when he leaves his house to his destination and when he gets out of his car we can confront him and ask about Daisy," suggested JoJo, when we were both seated in my private office.

"Won't work," I replied. "His bodyguard will just draw down on us or shoo us away or maybe hold us there for the police. The same would apply to going to his house and asking to speak to him. We wouldn't get anywhere near him, and if he has done in Daisy, as we suspect, our showing up will only alert him and put him on his guard. No, we'll have to trick him in some way but I'm damned if I can think of a way."

I had just lit up a cigar, sending JoJo into a fit of groans and eye rolling when it hit me like a bolt out of the blue. I had just thought of a way to at least get into Corning's presence and once there I could play it by ear. I picked up the receiver of my private phone and dialed "O" for the operator.

"Operator, how may I direct your call?"

"Yes, operator, I would like to speak to someone in public relations at Mammoth Studios in Hollywood," I rattled off.

"Do you know your party's name?"

"Not a clue, anyone in the PR department will do for a start."

"One moment please," replied the operator. But it was more than a moment before I was connected. In fact it was two or three minutes. Finally, I heard a phone ringing on the other end.

"Public relations, how may I help you?" a female voice answered.

"Yes, my name is Matthew Cole and I'm a private investigator. I need to speak to one of your PR people right away. It concerns one of your stars being intimately involved with a seventeen-year-old girl."

"Please hold a moment sir. I'll get someone for you," said the PBX operator at Paramount.

"What are you doing?" asked JoJo. "What's this about a teenaged girl?"

I blocked the mouthpiece with my palm and explained. "Movie actors can get themselves in all kinds of jams. It comes with their thinking that they're special and don't have to abide by the same rules as everybody else. The studios invest thousands of dollars in these stars and are deathly afraid of any scandal that could make them lose their investment. Sex with an underage girl is one of the worst no-nos imaginable in the eyes of studio execs."

"This is Oliver Thompkins. How may I help you Mr. Cole?"

"Yes, Mr. Tompkins, I am a private investigator. The parents of Gladys Prentiss, a young lady who just turned seventeen, have hired me to investigate a matter involving their daughter. It seems that during an argument, Gladys has broken down and told her mother that she and Alistair Corning have been having an affair. Apparently, they have been going at it like a pair of bunnies for about three months or so, according to Gladys. The parents want me to investigate and determine the truth of the matter."

"Would determining the truth of the matter involve the studio paying out a sum of money to the parents?" asked Tompkins, skepticism in his voice.

"Actually, no. Gladys's parents don't want any money. They are under no illusions about their daughter. You see, Gladys matured early. By the time she was fifteen she had boys swarming around her like shyster lawyers at a major car accident. People in the neighborhood began to refer to Gladys as the slut of Culver City. And then there was the time that the oversexed girl was caught naked behind the high school gym with the whole varsity football squad. No, the parents just want to know if she's lying about this whole thing, and, if she is, they're going to send her to live with her aunt in Boise."

"If they don't want money from us, then what do they want?" asked Tomkins.

"If I could be allowed to conduct a short private interview with Alistair Corning, I could probably clear this thing up pronto. I can guarantee that this matter will go no further and there will be no complications like press coverage or involving the police and such. I know this decision is probably above your pay grade so I don't expect a decision now. Call me back at WI 3-4582 when the studio is ready to discuss this further."

"Mr. Cole, let me talk this over with my superiors. I will get back to you within the hour," said Tompkins, and hung up.

"Do you think they will fall for it?" asked joJo.

"Probably. The scandal that would result from it getting out to the press that one of their stars was doing the dirty with an underage girl would be huge. It could drastically affect box office receipts and ultimately their bottom line. And money is truly all these guys care about," I answered, puffing on my cigar, the smoke giving JoJo fits.

About an hour later my phone rang. "A-1 DISCREET INVESTIGATIONS, Matthew Cole speaking," I said into the receiver.

"Yes, Mr. Cole, this is Oliver Tompkins. Would it be possible for you to come to the public relations department at the studio at one in the afternoon tomorrow to discuss this situation? Mr. Corning has indicated that he will be available to speak to you if it becomes necessary."

"Fine, Mr. Thompkins, I'll see you at one o'clock tomorrow," I said, and hung up the phone. Immediately after that, I jumped up and raised both hands above my head the way Joe Louis did after he knocked out Max Baer at the 3:09 mark in the fourth round.

§

The executive office complex at Mammoth Pictures was considerably nicer than it had been when I had last been there in

1944. I walked in and announced my name to the receptionist. From then on I was treated like royalty. A good looking blonde in a figure hugging black dress escorted me to an unoccupied office and asked if I wanted coffee or something stronger if I preferred. I declined the refreshment. Her bottom swayed out of the room and she left me alone. She must have had other parts that left with her but her bottom was the only part that I was looking at in that moment.

After a few minutes two men entered the room. One was young and fresh wearing a tweed jacket and bow tie. The other was older and stouter, wearing a dark suit with waistcoat and sporting a round red face. Both the men were clean shaven.

"Mr. Cole, my name is Arthur Hopkins. I'm the executive vice president in charge of public relations here at Mammoth," said the older man frowning. "My colleague is Oliver Tompkins, I believe you two spoke on the telephone." We all plastered phony smiles on our faces and shook hands all around like we were all old fraternity buddies. Hopkins acted so collegial that I thought for a minute that he was going to offer me a swig from the flask of bourbon in his hip pocket. Hopkins invited me to sit down and I sat in a stuffed chair while he and Tompkins occupied a sofa to my right.

"I'm sorry, Mr. Cole, but we think it ill advised to allow you to speak to Mr. Corning without us being present. I'm afraid this condition is non-negotiable," said Hopkins, talking like a lawyer, which I'm sure he was.

"If you two gentlemen will pardon the expression, let's cut the crap. Since our phone call yesterday you will have checked me out and discovered that I own one of the largest detective agencies in Southern California. I don't often handle cases myself, but Gladys' daddy is an old war buddy and I took this case as a favor to him. I would like to clear this case up fast by having a private, informal chat with Alistair Corning. But since you gentlemen don't seem to want to do this the easy way, I have no alternative but to report this matter to the police for investigation. And I'm sure it won't be long before the newspapers get ahold of the story," I said, starting to rise from my chair.

Arthur Hopkins, who had turned a deeper shade of red as I spoke, now raised his hands palms out. "Now, Mr. Cole, let's, not be too hasty. On second thought, I see no reason why you shouldn't be allowed to briefly speak privately to Mr. Corning, providing that I have your assurance that you will not make this matter public knowledge."

"You have my assurances," I replied. I could tell I had probably ruined Mr. Hopkins's digestion for about a week and a half. The poor bastard would probably go home and polish off the entire contents of his liquor cabinet.

"Mr. Tompkins and I will leave you now and send in Mr. Corning," Hopkins, said and the two men left.

The first thing I noticed about Alistair Corning when he burst into the room was that he was shorter and smaller than he appeared on the silver screen. But short male movie stars were common in Hollywood. Alan Ladd was only 5'6" and Humphrey Bogart was 5'8". The second thing I noticed about Corning was that he was madder than a spinster after someone stole the batteries out of her vibrator.

'What is the meaning of this?" growled Corning, in a clipped British accent, his face a mask of rage. "I don't know anyone named Gladys Prentiss and I don't have sex with teenaged girls!" The actor didn't sit down but just stood there five feet away from me with his hands balled into fists.

"Of course you don't. The tale about Gladys was just a made up story to allow me to get past your handlers and talk to you about something much more important."

"So this story that had me up all night fuming and pacing back and forth was a lie? Well, I don't see any reason to talk to you any further," said Corning, and turned to leave.

"I'm investigating the disappearance of Daisy Carter," I said quickly, before he could get to the door. "You might know her as Rhonda Faye."

Corning stopped in his tracks, turned, walked back and sat down on the same sofa the PR guys had recently vacated. "Rhonda is missing? I wondered why she didn't answer her phone," he said, in a much calmer voice.

'So you admit to knowing Rhonda Faye?" I asked.

"Sure I knew Rhonda. Up until about three weeks or a month ago we had a standing date every Saturday night."

"Rhonda's real name is Daisy Carter. I was hired by her boyfriend to find her after she went missing on a Saturday night about a month ago. I found written records in her apartment detailing all the men she was seeing and the dates she had been with them."

"So when you saw that I had many dates with Rhonda on Saturday nights, naturally you suspected me as having something to do with her disappearance. Right?" said Corning. "Well, I had nothing to do with it. By the way, what was the date of her disappearance?"

"October twentieth," I replied.

At this stage of my life I had become quite an expert on liars. In the span of my life I had been lied to by both my parents, some policemen, a Marine Corps recruiter, many, many women and assorted gangsters, just to name a few. I was also an accomplished liar, so I could usually tell when I was being lied to. I had a strong suspicion that Alistair Corning wasn't lying.

"In fact, I can prove I had nothing to do with this. On October twentieth I was in London on tour for the studio promoting my latest film, a ghastly, turgid little disaster named 'Highland Holiday.' And if you don't believe me, Life Magazine published a photograph of me three weeks ago posing on London Bridge"

"Okay, you're in the clear. Sorry for causing you all that anxiety," I said, sheepishly.

"When I walked in here I was mad enough to kill. Now all I can do is wish you God speed. I hope you find her. I like Rhonda a lot."

"Before I go, I've got a question. It's none of my business, but with you being a star I bet you have women crawling all over you on a daily basis. Why would you need to use the services of a call girl?" I asked.

'You're right, it's none of your business, but I'll tell you anyway. I do have women throwing themselves at me all the time. But very few of them will put up with my peculiar sexual proclivities. And the ones that will either want to marry me, want to use me to advance their career or can't keep their little mouths shut. I find it much less bother to just buy my sexual gratification."

On the way out of the room, I was confronted by the two PR men from Paramount.

"Everything has been cleared up just as I said it would. Mr. Corning is innocent of these charges. As for that little slut, Gladys, she doesn't know it yet but she'll be on the evening train up to Idaho," I said, and left.

CHAPTER FOURTEEN

WILSHIRE DISTRICT
LOS ANGELES
NOVEMBER 21, 1951
5:10 P.M.

"It's called tunnel vision," I said to JoJo. We were sitting in my office discussing my little adventure at Mammoth Pictures. "It's a problem that many detectives are susceptible to. You get excited following a trail of breadcrumbs and you exclude from your mind any evidence that points in another direction. Because Alistair was Daisy's regular Saturday night date, and he had a skull and crossbones symbol on his john book page I went after him exclusively without checking things out first and making sure of my facts. It's a good object lesson for you when you're out there investigating cases on your own."

"So where do we go from here?" she asked.

"We'll go back to the john book. We need to check out all the men on those pages. We'll start with the other guy with the poison symbol on his page."

We were interrupted by the buzzing of the intercom on my desk. I reached over and flipped a switch.

"Mr. Cole, there are two policemen at the front desk. They say they need to see you right away," said Betty the receptionist.

"Tell them to hang on, I'll be right out," I replied. I limped out to the reception desk and saw two men standing there. The first was a stocky, powerful guy in his mid-forties wearing a gray suit with vest and a gray felt fedora. The man's face was pasty white with bushy eyebrows and sagging jowls. The other man stood a little ways back behind the first. He was tall and thin wearing a blue suit and brown hat and was casually cleaning his teeth with a toothpick. Both men affected a posture of casual insolence. You could just tell from their demeanor that they thought they owned the world and could do pretty much anything they wanted to.

"You Cole?" asked the big guy, in an arrogant tone.

"Yep, that's me," I replied.

"Is there someplace we can talk? We got a problem that needs solving," said the large man, as he pulled aside the left lapel of his suit to reveal an LAPD badge pinned to his vest. "I'm Lt. Brandywine and this is Sgt. Connors. We're with the vice squad."

"Okay, follow me on back to my private office," I said, and led them past Betty's counter. Upon entering my office Lt. Brandywine saw JoJo standing beside my desk and asked, "Who's she?"

'This is Miss Marx, one of my detectives," I replied.

"Kinda looks like a Jewess don't she Ed?" asked the Lieutenant, directing the question to his partner.

"Yes, she does all right," replied Sgt. Connors.

Knowing Jojo as I did I braced for her response.

"Aw, shucks," she said, "you forgot to put your bedsheet and KKK hood back on this morning after you had sex with your sister."

The smirk on Brandywine's face was instantly replaced by a menacing scowl. "Don't you crack wise with me, girly, or I'll slap you silly," he uttered.

"Nobody is slapping anybody in my office unless I do the slapping. Say your piece Brandywine and then get out of here. Or maybe you want me to get on the line with Chief Parker. We're golfing buddies you know," I lied.

"We're just here to deliver a message. You was sniffin' round the Havana Club the other night, asking questions bout a girl named Daisy Carter. Some pretty tough people I know don't appreciate you sticking your nose in where it ain't wanted. I'm supposed to tell you that Daisy is fine and don't need your help. If you're smart you'll stop askin' folks bout her."

Our eyes locked for a few moments. When I didn't reply, he broke eye contact and sauntered out of my office followed by his skinny partner.

"That is about the most horrible, bigoted excuse for a human being I have ever had the misfortune to meet," said JoJo after the two cops left.

"Yeah, Lt. Brandywine appears to be a real winner alright. But worse than his personality is what his little visit implies. Up to now I have held out hope that Daisy Carter was still alive and whoever snatched her had her stashed somewhere. But I think that now we have to assume that she's dead. And someone rich or powerful enough to have two cops from the vice division in his pocket is willing to tip his hand to prevent anyone finding out what actually happened to her," I said. "Anyway, that's enough for today. First thing tomorrow morning we'll start checking out the list of johns in the little red book."

§

The next morning JoJo and I went through the list of phone numbers listed in Daisy's little red book again. For twelve of the numbers we had names and addresses as identified by the phone company. For the other thirteen numbers we only had the names of companies or corporations affiliated with them. I started calling these phone numbers acting on the premise that they were the private phone lines of big shots at these companies who liked to party with call girls. Regardless of who answered I told them all the same thing: "This is Western Union. We have an urgent telegram for Alexander Stephens." I thought it a safe bet that I wouldn't actually reach anyone by that name because the vice president of the Confederacy had been dead for ages and ages. The people who answered upon hearing my opening line would say things like "sorry, wrong number" or "there's no Stevens here." My next line was "Please, sir, the fate of a sick child is at stake. It's a matter of life and death that I reach Alexander Stephens. Who am I speaking to?" The perceived urgency of the call and the normal person's innate urge to be polite and helpful made it almost psychologically impossible for the guy on the line not to identify himself, if he didn't think about it too much before answering. Most of the Johns I called fell for it immediately and blurted out their names without hesitation. Three of them just hung up on me and I put a red "X" next to each of their numbers. I would circle back to them later if necessary.

By ten o'clock I had a handwritten list of twenty-one names to check out. I folded the list lengthwise and put it in my inside jacket pocket. "C'mon JoJo," I said, "Let's go over to the central library."

"Central library?" she repeated, with a puzzled look.

"We need to find a 1951 edition of a book called "The Los Angeles Business Index." The subtitle is "Who's who in business, government or entertainment in Southern California." It's a big ass heavy book. I almost ordered a copy for the office but the bastards who publish it want 150 bucks per copy. The central library will have a copy though," I said.

'You know, for a guy who has a gazillion dollars in the bank and who owns a thriving detective agency, you sure are cheap. This is the second time you have bitched about the price of a book to me," replied JoJo.

"Not cheap, just thrifty. I think it comes from all the times I struggled through life without having two nickels to rub together."

We piled into my Ford in front of my office. I backed the old heap out of its parking space and headed east on Wilshire. The late morning traffic was light. After about a block, I noticed that a big, black Buick or Oldsmobile had fallen in behind me three cars back and matched my speed. I couldn't tell how many people were inside the car, only that there was more than one. Whenever I changed lanes to go around a car turning right or left, the big black car matched my movements. I didn't tell JoJo that we had picked up a tail. I slowed and stopped at Flower and signaled with my left arm for a left turn. The big car followed my Ford through the turn. Now there were no other cars between mine and theirs.

The big black sedan suddenly sped up like it was going to pass me on the left. In astonishment I saw two different hands emerge from the passenger side of the sedan holding revolvers and a shotgun barrel with a magazine tube under it. I slammed on the brakes and came to a skidding stop.

"GET OUT NOW!" I shouted at JoJo while reaching across her body to mash down on the passenger door handle and shove her ahead of me out of the car and onto the pavement of the street. Continuing to move, I began to drag a bewildered JoJo toward the front of the Ford. "GET BEHIND THE ENGINE BLOCK," I shouted. We had barely arrived beside the right front tire when a multi-gun fusillade of shots sounded, along with the whang sounds of bullets striking sheet metal. This wasn't a movie scene, so I didn't act the hero and pull my gun, pop up and return fire. With this volume of fire it would have been suicide. No, I just hunkered down next to the tire holding JoJo in my arms to protect her as best I could from flying glass. I had been under fire a bunch of times during my service with the Marines on Guadalcanal during the war, so you might think I would handle it better than the average schlub. But the truth is, the second, tenth, or even the twentieth time you get shot at is just as scary as the first time.

Suddenly, the shooting stopped and I heard the sound of the big sedan accelerating away. I peeked around the front of my car in time to see the big car turning left on 6th Street at high speed. I didn't have time to get the license number.

JoJo and I stood and brushed ourselves off. I could tell that she was shaken and hyped up but to her credit she wasn't hysterical or panicky and didn't appear about to faint. I walked around my Ford and saw that it was a mess. Its driver's side was peppered with dozens of .38 caliber holes interspersed with the fist sized jagged holes that a 12 gauge shotgun makes when firing buckshot at close range. I limped back around to the other side of the car. None of the shots had penetrated the skin of the car on the passenger side. The heavy sheet metal on the driver's side of the Ford had apparently spent the force of the bullets. Jojo joined me on the driver's side of my mutilated Ford and gaped at the carnage.

"Well I guess we have just received a response from Mr. Jack Dragna," I said. "Look JoJo, up to now our discussions about the danger we are in have been theoretical. Now they just got real. Are you sure you don't want me to reassign you to another detective for your training."

JoJo looked at me like I'd lost my mind. "And let the bastards win? Never!" she said in a strong, clear voice. I was so proud of her that I almost hugged and kissed her right there beside my bullet riddled car. But I didn't do it, fearing she would think me an idiot.

The first cops to arrive at the shooting scene were two motorcycle officers. They were soon joined by a half a dozen cops in patrol cars. When the detectives showed up I told them I wouldn't talk to anyone but Lt. Miller in the chief's office. He arrived about forty-five minutes after the shooting.

"Sorry about this, Cole. Can you give us a description of any of the guys who shot at you?"

"Nope, I was too busy contorting myself into the shape of an automobile tire," I replied.

"The chief, when I told him about this incident, has authorized me to assign two officers to guard you around the clock. It's only fair seeing as how we got you into this."

I considered Miller's proposal for a few minutes. I really did. But I then declined his offer of protection. "Tell the chief I said thanks, but no thanks. I've got a job to do and some of the methods I use aren't always strictly legal. The last thing I need is two cops looking over my shoulder and putting the cuffs on me every time I step across some imaginary line."

My old Ford was hauled by a tow truck to the police impound yard as evidence. It was okay, the old heap wasn't drivable in its present condition anyway. Miller took JoJo and me in his car to city hall where we gave statements to a stenographer and were then let go. We took a cab to a used car lot on Pico that I had dealt with in the past. An hour later JoJo and I emerged driving a 1941 green Packard four door sedan with 38,000 miles on the odometer, that I had just purchased for two hundred bucks cash. The car had good rubber and the price included a full tank of gas.

JoJo and I arrived at the central library at a quarter after four, three hours after we had first started to go there. After some searching, I found a 1951 copy of The Los Angeles Business Index and set the heavy volume down on the top of a sturdy oak library table. While I started to look up names of the johns on the list, JoJo went to purchase coffee in paper cups from a disabled veteran's stand in the lobby of the library. By the time she returned with two steaming cups of black liquid, I told her I might have found out something interesting.

"You know the page on the john book that has the other red poison sign and the guy was listed as Mike C. by Daisy?" I asked JoJo. She nodded. "Well, listen to this. Quote: 'Michael Norton Conrad Jr. is the son of Michael Norton Conrad Sr., Los Angeles city councilman and president of MNC Industries, a defense contracting corporation with numerous facilities throughout the southland. Michael Norton Conrad Jr. is listed as a vice president at his father's corporation.'"

Inside my head, one of my remaining 383 brain cells suddenly came alive and held up a sign to another brain cell all the way on the other side of the cranium. The sign read: "connection!" in big red letters. The two brain cells began to force their way toward each other pushing aside and parting the crowd of other brain cells who were loafing around, drinking bourbon, smoking Lucky Strike cigarettes and just generally shooting the shit. Finally finding themselves together, the one with the sign asks the other, "Remember when Chief Parker was telling us about trying to get the city council to demote that bent captain in the vice division about a month ago and a councilman he thought he could count on suddenly switched his vote without explanation? Was that councilman named Conrad?"

"Yup," replied the other brain cell.

"A month ago? Right about the time Daisy disappeared?" asked the first brain cell.

"Yup," replied the other brain cell. He was a brain cell of few words.

CHAPTER FIFTEEN

FAIRFAX DISTRICT
LOS ANGELES
NOVEMBER 22, 1951
3:57 A.M.

The stink of cordite and rotten human flesh was in my nostrils as another wave of tough, fanatical Japanese soldiers emerged from the jungle sixty yards away and charged directly toward the depleted Marine lines. The Marine machine gun section to my right fed belt after belt of thirty caliber cartridges into their guns, laying down a tremendous volume of fire at the charging Japs and mowing them down in rows. But more Japanese soldiers emerged from the jungle, there seemed to be an endless supply, and the machine guns couldn't kill them fast enough. Choking down bile, I worked the bolt of my rifle and fired as fast as I could but was hampered with having to reload my rifle after each five rounds I fired. "Pickle" my foxhole mate didn't have that problem. He was armed with a Browning automatic rifle that fed from a magazine that held twenty rounds.

There was a lull in the fighting and the guns fell silent. I began checking my gear and preparing for the next wave of Japanese. I noticed that I was almost out of ammunition. Then I felt the presence of someone behind me. I looked back and saw Helga, the Viking Queen standing behind my hole in her Swedish farm girl outfit, blonde pigtails and all.

"Why didn't you bring more ammunition with you? Are you stupid? I can't understand what my daughter sees in you," she blurted out, almost shouting.

"Helga, dammit, shut the fuck up or you'll draw Japanese fire." I whispered hoarsely.

"Nonsense, as my uncle Ole used to say, 'Preparation prevents regret and recriminations.'"

"Fine! Go ahead and shout all you want, I hope a Jap sniper drills you between the eyes you cantankerous bitch," I said, losing my temper.

"Well, it's been nice talkin to ya," said Helga as she displayed an evil grin and strolled off.

I turned back to the battle and was astonished to see multiple Jap grenades arcing through the air directly toward my hole, leaving little wisps of smoke trailing behind them. I tried catching and throwing them back as they sailed in but there were too many of them for me to handle. One grenade slipped from my fingers and dropped into the bottom of the hole and there was a tremendous roar and a white hot, blinding flash.

I sat up in bed soaked in sweat even though it was a chilly November night. I rose from the bed and staggered to the closet where I put on my robe. Limping down the hall to my den, I immediately took two large pulls on the neck of a bottle of Jack Daniel's Old Number 7 Whiskey and lit up a Lucky Strike. Thus fortified, I sat in my easy chair and waited for my respiration and heartbeat to come down to normal.

Prior to that night I hadn't had any war dreams in over a year. I kind of understood why I had one tonight, what with the shooting yesterday. But what the hell was Helga, the Viking Queen doing invading my dreams? If this turned out to be a regular occurrence, I would just have to end it all.

My old buddy Jack Daniels did his magic. My respiration and heart rate soon returned to normal levels. But I was too keyed up to even try to fall asleep again. Unbidden, I relived in my mind the attempted assassination of JoJo and me the day before. My hands clenched and unclenched repeatedly as I experienced again the gut wrenching terror I felt during the attack while JoJo and I crouched there on the street trying to use the engine block of my car as cover.

Captain Straight: "You were lucky. If you hadn't looked in the rear view mirror when you did and saw those guns sticking out the window of that car, June would be planning your funeral about now."

My pulse rate started to rise again and I knew I would have to force my mind to think about something else or my nerves would never settle down. My mind turned to the case of Daisy Carter.

At the library the previous afternoon, after discovering that one of the johns JoJo and I were investigating was the son of a Los Angeles city councilman, I went ahead and looked up the other names on our list of Daisy's clients. Most of them were well to do businessmen and executives for various Los Angeles companies and corporations. It was possible that this group of highly positioned men harbored a monster capable of murdering a woman and then attempting to cover it up, but I doubted it. One of the johns on the list was a professional gambler. He travelled form high stakes poker game to high stakes poker game throughout California and Nevada and availed himself of Daisy's services when he was in Los Angeles. I guess he was a possible. If Michael Conrad, son of the councilman, didn't pan out we would give this guy a closer look.

The problem I had at this stage of the investigation was how to get close enough to Michael Norton Conrad, Jr. to find out anything. If he was a killer, it would stand to reason that he would be on his guard and suspicious of anyone sniffing around him for information. I decided that I would somehow get within his circle of contacts, deliberately stir the pot and see what happened.

I must have dozed off for a while because before I knew it it was six a.m. and June was standing in the doorway of my den in her bathrobe with tousled hair and carrying Winston on her hip.

My baby boy was giving me the evil eye and looking especially surly this morning.

"Well, this is new," she said, "did you get up early to help me scrub your son's cereal spatters off the kitchen ceiling? Or maybe before you go to work we can pull the waist high weeds growing out of control next to the back door. We can gaze longingly into each other's eyes while we murder dandelions and bull thistle without mercy."

She was lying about the weeds. They weren't waist high at all, only about mid-thigh. "I had a nightmare and couldn't get back to sleep," I replied to her.

"War dreams again?"

"Yeah, but this time there was a new twist. The Viking Queen was in this one and she scared me more than the charging waves of bloodthirsty Japs," I answered.

On my way out the door about 7:45, June stopped me.

"You have to be home no later than five tonight. My parents are coming over for dinner;" she said, without even a hint of shame.

'Oh, I'm sorry sugar, but I can't be here tonight." I said. "I have to fly to Moscow and consult with Uncle Joe Stalin to try to find a way of removing Beria as head of the NKVD. Stalin thinks the crazy bastard is getting a little too big for his britches."

"Wait a minute, Stalin? That's the lamest excuse I have ever heard. You can come up with a something better than that."

"No, really, Stalin and I are old pals. In the mid-twenties when things weren't going well in the Soviet Union and they were constantly running out of toilet paper, Stalin would clandestinely slip out of Russia every six months or so and come to stay at the Hollywood Roosevelt Hotel and register under the name of Joe Vissarionovich. I was about ten then and I would shine his shoes and we would talk about politics. He ended up teaching me a major life lesson," I said.

"And what ,pray tell, what was this major life lesson Josef Stalin taught you?" asked June, with raised eyebrows.

"Communists are lousy tippers."

'Are you through?" asked June.

"Yes."

"Well, old Uncle Joe will just have to do without you. Be here before five or I'll give my mother the key to your liquor cabinet and she might just pour the contents of all the bottles into one big jug."

§

In the whole six plus years my detective agency had been located in our office on Wilshire Boulevard; I had never once arrived for work before 9:45 a.m. although the office opened for business at 8. Caroline Adderley usually came in about 9. But Caroline and I trusted our employees not to goof off in the hour or so before she arrived.

So I was a little surprised at the scene that I confronted when I limped in the door at 8:10 a.m. Betty the receptionist had a cup of coffee and two glazed doughnuts sitting in front of her on the front counter. She was leaning back on her stool with her feet on the typewriter stand beside her and was talking to a friend on the headset of her PBX machine.

"No, I haven't done any Christmas shopping yet. We don't know yet how big our bonus will be this year," I overheard her say.

Across the room Caroline's jittery assistant, Luann, was sitting at her desk lost in the pages of a romance novel. I could hear laughter coming from the open door of the bullpen indicating the detectives were goofing off too.

"AHEM," I uttered loudly.

Betty turned her head toward me and Luann looked up from her book at the same time. Their eyes also widened in unison and both exploded up from their seats quicker than Dorothy's aunt's farmhouse when it was snatched up by the tornado. "Oh, Mr. Cole, I didn't see you there," said Betty, with one palm covering her mouth. Instantly it seemed the office was transformed into the bustling normalcy of any work day. It must have been psychic communication of some sort, kind of like that eerie mental telepathy that occurs between women whenever there's a 50 % off sale on dresses at May Company.

"Obviously," I replied. "Do you have any idea what would happen if I told Mrs. Adderley about what I saw just now?"

"Yes, sir," answered Betty, her face going pale.

"I'll make a deal with you," I said to her with a grin. "Give me one of those doughnuts and you'll buy my silence forever."

JoJo Marx came in about 9:15 a.m. From a seated position behind my desk, I gave her a stern look. "So I've been sitting here for hours trying to get a handle on how to proceed in the Carter case. I desperately needed my partner's input but she wasn't here to help me," I said.

"I very seldom lower myself by swearing, but in this instance nothing else is appropriate. You're as full of shit as a Christmas turkey. What happened? Did your wife throw you out for telling bad jokes again?" asked JoJo.

"Something like that. Anyway, I woke up early and couldn't get back to sleep. Have you given any thought to how we nail this councilman's son if he's the one we're looking for?"

"He has that house in Laurel Canyon on Laurel Pass Avenue. We could pretend to be building inspectors or something and pull the little key in the clay trick we played on that apartment manager. That house is probably where the murder took place if he's the guy and if it was a murder," answered JoJo.

"No, that won't work. He'll have servants there all the time and we won't get access to a door key. We'll have to think of something else," I said, and paused for a moment.

Then a lightbulb lit up inside my head, bells clanged and Elmer Fudd cried "Hooway." "I've got it. The way in to this guy is through his old man," I said, picked up the receiver of my private phone and dialed "O."

"Operator, number please."

"Yes, operator, connect me with Councilman Michael Conrad's office in city hall." While I waited for the call to be connected, I drummed my fingers on the top of my desk, eliciting a frustrated and bug eyed look from Jojo

"Councilman Conrad's office," answered a delectable female voice.

"Yes. My name is Matthew Cole. I was wondering if it might be possible to speak to the councilman's political director."

"Just a moment, Mr. Cole, I'll locate him," said the delicious voice.

"This is Jack Brooks. How may I help you Mr. Cole." The voice was friendly and smooth, very smooth.

"Yes, Mr. Brooks, first let me say that I have been an admirer from afar of Mr. Conrad's masterly leadership on the council. The world needs more men like him in positions of authority. And secondly, my father left me a considerable sum of money some years ago when he died. I have in mind a building project utilizing a large part of my inheritance. The project might be considered by some to be controversial and I figured that the odds of my getting approval for my venture would be considerably enhanced if I had a friend in city hall. As a gesture to show my admiration for Councilman Conrad, I would be willing to contribute in a tangible way to his campaign fund."

"Mr. Cole, could you excuse me for just a moment? I won't be long," asked Brooks.

"Surely," I answered.

About two minutes later, Brooks was back on the line, his voice even friendlier. "Sorry to keep you waiting. Are you the Matthew Cole who is the heir to the Cole's Mustard fortune?" The bastard had probably looked me up on some secret list of all the millionaires in Los Angeles.

"One in the same," I replied.

"Well in that case, Mr. Cole, let me tell you how happy the councilman will be when I tell him that you called. In fact, your timing couldn't have been more auspicious. The councilman is holding a private reception for friends and donors to his campaign at his home tomorrow at two p.m. The address is 1348 Stone Canyon Road in Bel Air. I do hope you can attend."

"May I bring my assistant along?" I asked.

"Yes, sir, that will be fine."

CHAPTER SIXTEEN

BEL AIR
LOS ANGELES
NOVEMBER 22, 1951
2:10 P.M.

I studied the large Greek revival style house as I drove my Cadillac up the wide circular driveway. The six fluted columns on its façade made it look like the main house of Twelve Oaks plantation in the movie "Gone with The Wind". I half expected at any minute to see Scarlett O'Hara come flouncing out the front door in a pretty gown followed by all her handsome, southern beaus.

"How are we going to handle this?" asked JoJo who was sitting in the passenger seat. She had dressed for the part as a personal assistant to a tee, wearing her blue business suit with her hair pulled back into a tight bun. As a finishing touch she had gotten some big horn rim glasses with clear lenses from somewhere. They gave her makeup free face a studious, mousy appearance.

"I know it's hard for you to do, but let me do the talking," I answered. Our eyes met and she nodded her head. Her large eyes were dancing with amusement. I could tell she was having a grand time.

At the top of the driveway I was met by a uniformed parking attendant who ran around the car and opened the door for JoJo. He then ran back around and did the same for me as well as giving me a numbered ticket.

As we were walking toward the front door of the mansion, I noticed that JoJo, carrying a briefcase as a prop, was walking by my left side, but a little behind me. Again, this was perfectly in character for a personal assistant. The girl was a born actress. Even though I hadn't coached her on how to play her part, she was nailing it. She was subtly telling everyone around her that she wasn't a wife or even a girlfriend, just a humble employee.

When we entered the foyer of the house I was suitably impressed. The floor was of white and black marble tiles laid in a brick pattern. Two magnificent wide curving staircases on each side of an arch emptied onto the floor. A crowd of obviously well off people crowded the foyer. I might have been mistaken but for a moment I thought I saw Ashley Wilkes's cousin from Atlanta, Melanie Hamilton, fanning herself while speaking to that dashing rogue from Charleston, Capt. Rhett Butler.

"Hello, you must be Matthew Cole. My name is Jack Brooks," said a tall trim man in a finely tailored suit, as he walked up to me and stuck out his hand. He was in his early forties, I would say, with dark brown pomaded hair, a pencil thin mustache and a direct gaze. Everything about him said upper crust and proud of it. How he picked me out in the crowd is a mystery, unless in the time since our phone call the day before he had dug up a photograph of me somewhere.

"Nice to meet you. This is my assistant, Miss Marx," I said, while shaking his hand. JoJo only nodded and looked at the floor like she was embarrassed by the attention. "You'll have to forgive my assistant. She doesn't speak much because her teeth are all jagged and crooked and they make her sound like Donald Duck when she talks," I said as I glanced around at my surroundings. "Wow, nice place your boss has here."

"Yes, it is magnificent isn't it? Of course Mr. Conrad could never afford a house like this on a councilman's salary. He is also founder and president of MNC Industries. His company made him a fortune selling combat gear to the government during the big war and is still adding to his net worth during the smaller present one in Korea. The company makes web gear, belts, magazine pouches, canteen covers, rifle slings, knapsacks and items like that."

"Is the councilman married and does he have any children?" I asked, already knowing the answer.

"Tragically, Mrs. Conrad succumbed to breast cancer about ten years ago. But the councilman has a son he is extremely proud of who serves as vice president of his company," said Brooks. I wonder, I thought, how proud the councilman would be if he knew his son was out roughing up call girls and might be a murderer.

"I'll tell you a little secret," continued Jack Brooks, "Michael Conrad Jr. might be elevated to the presidency of the company much sooner than we all thought. There is some conversation in high political circles around the state about running the councilman for Lieutenant Governor on the Republican ticket in the election two years hence. This might be your opportunity to get in on the ground floor, so to speak, with your financial support. Having the Lieutenant Governor of California as a special friend is certainly much better than a city councilman."

"That's certainly food for thought, Mr. Brooks. I'll consider it," I replied.

"Call me Jack,' said Brooks. 'Say, would you like to meet Councilman Conrad?"

"It would be an honor," I replied.

"Follow me. I'll take you to him," said Brooks, and turned on his heel. I only staggered a little bit when JoJo kicked me surreptitiously but sharply on my right calf as he led us through the arch between the two stairways and to a smaller room off the hallway. It was a ballroom or some such with a parquet oak floor and was bare of furniture except for a string quartet in a corner playing Mozart softly and sedately.

In the center of the room holding court was the great man himself, Michael Norton Conrad Sr. He was slightly under six feet tall with an enormous head and reminded me of Lionel Barrymore. Conrad's angular tanned and lined face looked distracted, like he didn't really want to be where he was, although he appeared relaxed and self-assured. His full head of wavy, mostly salt and pepper hair had gone entirely gray at the temples giving him a distinguished look. He appeared to be the kind of guy who would show up at a casting call for an actor to play a role as an ambassador to the Court of St, James. His conservatively cut and tailored tweed Saville Row suit must have cost him five hundred dollars to import from London if it cost a dime.

"Councilman Conrad, I'd like you to meet Mr. Matthew Cole, heir to the Cole's Mustard fortune. I think he might be persuaded to climb aboard our train," said Jack Brooks, as we approached the politician. Conrad smiled and held out his hand and I grasped it. His shake was firm and dry but his smile was phony. I could tell by the eyes, they were cold as ice. I didn't introduce my assistant this time around. Great men weren't interested in the riff-raff and besides, I didn't want another kick from JoJo.

"Well Mr. Cole, Jack tells me that you are thinking of getting aboard our little political train. If you do, I can assure you that the future looks bright and abounding in opportunities." What's with the train metaphor, I thought. It sounded cheesy to me.

"Yes, councilman, I'm considering a substantial contribution to your campaign. You see, my two partners and I are considering a multimillion dollar project that might need a little help from city hall to accomplish," I said.

"Oh, who are your partners? Maybe I know them."

"Rhonda Faye and Daisy Carter," I said, and waited for a reaction. And boy did I get a reaction. Conrad's eyes expanded to the size half dollars and his whole body jumped like he had been slapped. His angry eyes bored into me.

The Brat: "Wow, this son of a bitch might as well have taken off all his clothes and jumped up and down with a lit road flare tied to his peter."

"Who are you? No, wait. Follow me, we'll have this conversation in private," said the councilman. He took off out of the room with JoJo and me following. He led us further down the hall to another room, this time a study. I noticed that it was a dandy room paneled in dark walnut with red leather furniture and smelling of fine cigars, single malt whiskey, money and privilege. Conrad seated himself behind a massive desk but left JoJo and I to stand in the middle of the room.

"You're here under false pretenses. I could have you arrested," said the councilman, angrily.

"No, that won't work for you," I answered. "I'm who I told your political fixer I was. I'm Matthew Cole and I truly am the heir to the Cole's Mustard fortune as Jack Brooks called it. I also own a detective agency and we're investigating the disappearance of a call girl employed by the Havana Club going by the stage name of Rhonda Faye but whose real name is Daisy Carter. We have developed evidence that your son was one of Daisy's regular customers. We also know from a secret record she kept of her client's quirks that your son's sexual tastes run to inflicting pain and choking the women he has sex with. Your boy, up until a few minutes ago was just one of several suspects in her disappearance. Your reaction in the other room to my repeating Daisy's names has catapulted him to a position as the number one suspect. If he didn't have anything to do with Daisy's disappearance, then why would you be so familiar with her name?"

A uniformed maid suddenly opened the door and stepped into the room. She was about fifty with gray hair and she had a distressed, worried look on her face. Maybe her feet hurt or something. "You rang for me sir," she said. Conrad must have pushed a secret button to summon her.

"Doris, show these people out. I have no wish to talk to them further," said the councilman, and swiveled his chair around so his back was to us.

As I was driving back down the driveway toward Stone Canyon Road, JoJo asked me a question. "What did you accomplish in your conversation with Conrad? It seems to me that you gave away everything and got nothing in return."

"What we have just done in there is the equivalent of a farm boy knocking a hornet's nest off a limb of a pear tree and then running like hell to avoid being stung. We shall see if we, like the boy, are able to escape or if we end up being caught and stung by the angry hornets."

CHAPTER SEVENTEEN

WILSHIRE DISTRICT
LOS ANGELES
NOVEMBER 22, 1951
3:45 P.M.

I was headed east on Wilshire about a block away from my office when a black and white 1950 Ford police cruiser fell in behind me and the uniformed policeman driving it activated his forward shining red light. I obediently pulled to the curb and stopped. The passenger officer, also in uniform, got out of the police car and approached my driver's side window.

"Just sit tight for a while. There's somebody that wants to talk to you. He'll be here soon," said the officer and walked back to the prowl car and got back in.

"What do you think this is all about?" asked JoJo.

"I think the hornets are swarming sooner than we thought."

About fifteen minutes later another 1950 Ford sedan pulled up and stopped behind the police car. It was identical to the marked police car except the cop car had white painted doors, light cans on the roof and a big, chrome siren mounted on the left front fender. I could see three men in hats occupying the plain car as the driver stuck his arm out of his window and waved to the two uniformed policemen. The patrol cops waved back and then drove away. Next, I saw the driver of the plain black car get out and approach my Cadillac. I wasn't shocked to see that it was Lt Brandywine's skinny partner, Sgt. Connors, walking toward my window.

"Captain Reed wants to talk to you," said Connors, while jerking his thumb toward the black car.

"Why don't you ask Captain Reed to come up here and sit in my car. It's much more comfortable," I suggested.

"Cut the gab, let's go," replied Sgt. Connors.

I reluctantly got out and walked back to the black car. Oh well, I thought, so much for Chief Parker's wire recorder. I got in the back on the right, with Captain Reed sitting across the backseat from me. He was old for a cop, maybe sixty or so and was wearing a navy blue seersucker suit and drab tie. His fedora was tilted back on his head revealing the front part of a mostly bald head. His head appeared too large for his body, almost to the point of being a caricature. The most prominent features on his face were hanging jowls and a big nose, both shot through with little purple veins. Without having to ask, I knew by the veins that Reed was very fond of the booze.

"For a gumshoe with a gimpy leg you sure can stir up trouble," began Reed, his voice hoarse and raspy. He probably smoked too many cigars as well as overconsuming alcoholic beverages.

"Do you have any idea what a hullabaloo you caused among our high class betters with your little visit to Bel Air this afternoon?" asked the bent cop. "Councilman Conrad and his son are apoplectic and Jack Dragna's not far behind them."

"Just doing my job. I think that Conrad's son beat to death a missing woman that I was hired to find. The councilman knows about it and he's trying to cover it up to protect his asshole son."

"This girl we're talking about that you're trying so hard to find was named Daisy Carter? Well, Daisy Carter was a whore," said Reed.

"What's that have to do with it," I asked back.

"Whores come and whores go. Whores live and whores die. What's a dead whore matter in the great scheme of things?" I decided then and there that I didn't like Captain Reed very much.

"You're wrong. The death of this one does matter. Daisy didn't deserve being choked to death by a vicious pampered swell just as she was contemplating leaving the business and cleaning up her life," I answered.

"Sentimentality in this modern world is a serious weakness, one that's probably going to get you killed, and it could be today," said the crook wearing a badge. I remained silent and didn't answer him.

"So my problem now is what I'm going to do with you. Michael Conrad and his son want me to mash you like a bug. Jack Dragna wants you dead because he thinks you might put the kibosh on one of his prostitution operations and because he thinks you're working with Mickey Cohen's mob against him. And if you're the typical gumshoe, you've probably made tons of enemies who also want you on a slab in the morgue, but dealing with you has also put me into a bit of a quandary."

"You see," continued Reed, "the word around town is that you are a guy able to get private messages to the leadership of the Cohen organization. I've had a business relationship with Jack Dragna for at least fifteen years but I also am seeing which way the winds are blowing. I think that Mickey Cohen has the stronger hand and is going to win out over Dragna eventually. I want you to tell Cohen's people that I'm willing to transfer my loyalty to them for a price. Dragna is paying me a grand a week. If Cohen is willing to go a grand-and-a-half, I'm in. So there's my quandary. Jack Dragna and Councilman Conrad would prefer you to disappear, but you're Cohen's guy and I need to keep you alive long enough to deliver my message to him. So here's the deal, drop the investigation into Daisy Carter's disappearance and deliver my message. If you do that, I let you live, at least for a while. You Okay with that?"

"Okay, sure," I lied.

"I see you're still going around with that little loud mouthed Jewess. Why? Does she give good head?" asked Lt. Brandywine from his position in the front passenger seat. I didn't answer him.

I opened the back door of the police detective car and rejoined JoJo in my Cadillac. The black Ford made a U-turn and headed west on Wilshire. I quickly brought JoJo up to speed on the conversation I had just had with Reed.

"Are you going to deliver Reed's message to Cohen?" asked JoJo.

"Yeah probably. I have so little regard for Captain Reed that at any other time I wouldn't piss on him if he was on fire, however, in this case it suits my purpose. But it also opens up a golden opportunity that I need to discus with Lt. Miller in Chief Parker's office."

Back in my office, I made two phone calls. The first was to the number "Johnny Stomp" Stompanato had given me in his car. When the phone was picked up on the other end, I identified myself and asked for Stompanato. While I waited, I heard the sounds of glasses clinking together and a woman laughing drunkenly. Finally, the phone was picked up and a voice I recognized as that of the mob boss came on the line.

"This is Johnny. Okay gumshoe, whacha got?"

"I just got contacted by Captain Brian Reed, head of the vice division. He told me he's ready to abandon Dragna and come over to Cohen's side. He said he wants a grand-and-a-half a week to play for your team."

"Well imagine that, the captain of the vice division. I'll talk this over with Mickey and let you know," said Stompanato, and hung up.

The second call was to Chief Parker's office in city hall. I asked for Lt Miller and waited about five minutes for him to come on the line.

"Lieutenant Miller."

"This is Matt Cole. There's been a development. I was driving down the street today when I was stopped by a black and white with two cops in it. A little later Captain Reed and his two crooked buddies, Brandywine and Connors, show up and want to talk to me. I tried but wasn't able to get Reed to sit in my car and talk so I couldn't get a recording of our conversation. But the upshot is this: Reed wanted me to communicate with Mickey Cohen and tell him that the captain was graciously willing to transfer his allegiance from Dragna to Cohen for a grand-and-a-half a week. I've already passed on the message to Johnny Stompanato.

"Fat lot of good it does us though if we don't have any proof," replied Miller.

"Well, I've come up with an idea that might just solve your little problem with Captain Reed. I suggest that you activate that fifty thousand watt rumor mill of yours. You know, the one that almost got me killed, and tell the world that our beloved bent captain has offered to turn his coat. Jack Dragna will be apoplectic when he hears about this development and might just solve the Captain Reed problem for you permanently."

"Actually, that's not a bad idea. I'll talk to Chief Parker about it but I don't think he will have a problem with it," said Miller.

After I hung up the phone I looked at JoJo, who was sitting across the desk from me looking exhausted. It had been a hell of a day. "JoJo, go home." I said. "That's enough for one day. Why don't you and your new boyfriend go out and have some fun tonight, see a movie or something?"

"It's none of your business what my boyfriend and I do or don't do," she replied. Oh well, I thought, she'll never be the warm and fuzzy kind of girl.

I glanced at my watch. "Oh, shit! I only have a half hour to get home before the Viking Queen is handed the key to my liquor cabinet," I blurted out.

"What?" asked JoJo.

"Never mind."

§

When I walked in the front door of my house, my nostrils were suddenly overwhelmed by the delectable aroma of roasting dead cow flesh. My mouth started to water uncontrollably to the point that I had to wipe some saliva that tried to escape from the corners of my mouth with the thumb and index finger of one hand.

The first person I saw after entering was June's Aunt Ingrid, Helga's slightly younger sister. She was carrying a tray of pickles from the kitchen to the dining room table. Although my mother-in-law Helga and Ingrid were supposedly biological sisters, they couldn't have looked less alike. While Helga was blonde and tall and built like a brick shithouse, Ingrid was as tall but skinny as a rail and had dark hair. She resembled Jack's beanstalk without the leaves. While not very well endowed in the brains department in the first place, a few years ago Ingrid suffered a nervous breakdown resulting in her doctor putting her on happy pills for life. She stumbled around in a fog most of the time saying the goofiest things. If confronted with the news that a rogue planet in outer space had slipped its orbit and was careening toward the earth and about to hit and extinguish all life in ten minutes, Ingrid would ask, "Ooh, what color is it." She did have one habit that endeared her to me, however. She chain smoked Chesterfield cigarettes, not stopping even during meals. Wherever she went she trailed a cloud of blue tinted smoke. The habit caused her sister and niece to lose their minds in exasperation, taking some of the heat off me.

"Hello, Ingrid, I didn't know you and Frank were going to be here. Welcome," I said. Frank was Ingrid's husband. A guy in his sixties and balding, he wore his pants pulled up to just under his nipple line and was a man of very few words. In fact, if I ever got five words out of Frank throughout a whole evening I would consider it a victory and reward myself with an extra shot of Jack Daniel's, Old No.7 Whiskey.

Ingrid took another puff on her Chesterfield before looking at me with her characteristic out-of-focus expression. "Oh, hello Matthew, so glad you could come."

I was about to remind Ingrid that I was in my own house, but before I could say anything June walked into the room from the kitchen. She was all dolled up in a stunning, blue cocktail dress and looked like a million bucks. My beautiful wife approached me and gave me an affectionate kiss on the lips.

"Promise me that you will behave yourself tonight. I don't want you to provoke my mother like you did the last time we had them over," she admonished, in a casual voice but one with steel backing it up.

"I'm not promising anything. If the Viking Queen needles me like the last time she was here and backs me into a corner, I'll bite back at her like a cornered Republican. Where is her royal highness anyway?" I asked.

"She's in the kitchen fussing about the roast in the oven. She's been here since two o'clock helping me cook dinner and taking care of Bobby," she answered. This was typical of the Viking Queen's modus operandi. My wife was a wonderful cook and perfectly capable of preparing a superb roast beef dinner on her own. But Helga just couldn't bring herself to trust in her daughter's competence. No, she had to come over here three hours early and stand over June all day supervising her like a schoolmarm instructing the class idiot.

And then, speak of the devil, Helga Lindstrom, all 180 pounds of sinew, gristle, bad temper and muscle and wearing a paisley print dress, emerged from the kitchen carrying my boy Winston. Our eyes locked.

"Good evening, Matthew," she said, displaying a phony, insincere smile.

"Hello Helga," I answered back, displaying a phony, insincere smile.

Like the moment the natives bring the bound and gagged missionaries out of the witch doctor's hut and prepare to throw them into the big iron pot, the tension in the room started to build. Before long it was crackling and sizzling like the atmosphere in one of Nikola Tesla's electro-erotic fever dreams. Even Winston felt it. He put that adorable expression on his face that he usually reserved for when he was about to shoot a huge load of baby shit into his diaper. My boy reacted to the unpleasant aura around him by putting his arms around Helga's neck, and she flashed me a triumphant smile, a genuine one this time.

My mother-in-law always made a point to crow about my son Winston preferring her to me. I contended that things weren't exactly as they appeared to be. Winston loved to breastfeed. In fact it was his favorite activity and he was constantly, night and day, pestering my wife to whip out a nipple. He would rather breastfeed than pick three winning horses and win the trifecta at Hollywood park. Well, maybe not the trifecta, but at least the exacta. So whenever Helga walks in our door with her enormous breasts straining the fabric of her dress, Winston looks at those enormous baby milk tanks and flashes an expression on his face like he had just rediscovered the Lost Dutchman gold mine. And of course, because he was after al just a baby with only a partially developed ability to remember things, he fell for it every time.

June, getting tired of watching us glare at each other, intervened. "Why don't you pour a drink and go sit down in your den until dinner's ready. Daddy and Frank are already in there." she suggested. I nodded to her and headed for the kitchen where I got down from a shelf my extra-large glass tumbler, the one I kept reserved for emergencies like earthquakes, floods, impending meteorite impacts and Helga coming to my house, and filled it to the brim with Jack Daniel's bourbon from my liquor cabinet. Thus fortified, I limped off toward my den.

CHAPTER EIGHTEEN

FAIRFAX DISTRICT
LOS ANGELES
NOVEMBER 22, 1951
5:30 P.M.

My father-in-law Warren along with Frank were sitting in my den when I ambled in the door. Frank was in my favorite easy chair with his hands folded in his lap. He was sitting absolutely still with only his eyes moving like a frog squatting on a lily pad waiting for an unsuspecting fly to get within tongue range.

"Hello, Frank," I said.

"Low," answered Frank. He wasn't overly fond of words of more than one syllable.

"Hello Warren."

"Why, hello, Matt. Thank you for having us over," said Warren. He was a little guy in his fifties who was half the size of his wife Helga. He was balding on top, wore a bushy mustache and unfortunately had been born with a weak chin. I had often told June that he should shave off the mustache and grow a beard like a Russian Cossack to hide the weak chin. Warren worked at the western office of a federal government agency called the Rural Electrification Project in Los Angeles as some kind of bean counter. As to why the government would locate the western office of the Rural Electrification Project in a city of millions of people that had been electrified since 1910, I had no idea.

I sat down on the unoccupied portion of the sofa with Warren, put my feet up on the coffee table and took a sip of my bourbon.

"Say, Matt, I wanted to tell you. Ivan has come up with an invention that will revolutionize kitchens across the country. With say three thousand dollars you could get in on the ground floor." said Warren. Ivan was my father-in-law's crackpot next door neighbor. He was an inveterate tinkerer and inventor. Warren was his biggest booster and fund raiser.

"I don't know, Warren," I replied, "remember what happened with Ivan's 'friction potato peeler' you got me to invest in a few months ago?" The "friction potato peeler" sounded like a good idea at the time. It was a sturdy canister that held six or seven russet potatoes attached to an electric motor that would violently agitate the contraption. The friction of the potatoes rubbing together under a jet of water would in theory remove the peels. And it worked after a fashion, but with one teeny little problem.

One of the potatoes would invariably come out white, clean and glistening. The other six would emerge the size of marbles.

"I know, that one didn't work out, but this new idea is pure genius," answered Warren.

"Okay, tell me about it."

'It's a dishwasher that cleans dishes and silverware with sulphuric acid," said Warren proudly.

Captain Straight: "Let's see, cleaning dishes with sulphuric acid, what could go wrong?"

"I'm sorry, Warren, but I think I'll pass on this one," I answered. "Frank, what do you think?"

"No, dumb idea," he replied and I almost fell off the sofa. Frank had just strung three words together to form a sentence fragment. To celebrate this red letter occasion, I drained my tumbler of bourbon and went to get a refill.

At a quarter to seven June appeared at the door of my den to announce that dinner was ready and we all trooped to the dining room. When I entered the room I was dumbfounded. The sturdy oak table was groaning under the weight of a veritable sea of food. There was a roast the size of a small delivery truck. What looked like twin winemaker's vats were heaped full of mashed potatoes and gravy. There was a salad bowl the size of Rhode Island, and about ten gallons of peas with tiny little cubes of carrot mixed in, oceans of green beans, and last but not least, an estuary of creamed corn. Okay, maybe I'm exaggerating just a wee bit, but let's just say that there was enough food on that table to feed six people directly and one baby indirectly for a month.

We all sat down. June and I had the end spots. Ingrid and Frank were on one side and Helga and Warren were on the other. My boy Winston was tucked between Helga and June in his high chair and he didn't look happy at all. By this time of the evening he had figured out that those two enormous baby milk tanks that Helga had attached to her chest that he had been so ecstatic about earlier were in reality as empty as the Sun Valley ski slopes in August. He was gazing at her the same way the Lone Ranger looked at Tonto that time the sidekick wasn't careful enough with his spear while riding behind him.

Warren then gave the blessing. He delivered the same canned prayer he always did, full of "thees" and "thous." I suspected that the Almighty had a good laugh at people like Warren who thought they couldn't communicate with Him except in the language of the sixteenth century. After all, he was the Almighty. I'm sure he kept up on current trends in the English language. We then started to pass the dishes around and fill our plates. As usual, Helga hadn't trusted me to carve the roast properly so she had done it in the kitchen before she brought it to the table.

Winston started to fuss. He made a grab for each bowl of food as it was passed by him. I'm sure he didn't know what was in those dishes but he wanted his share of the stuff everyone else was stuffing in their mouths. Helga steered the bowls just out of his reach and he got madder and madder. "Oh, no, Bobbykins, grandma's little boy can't have big people food," said Helga. Red in the face, Winston stared up at her with murder in his eyes- like the time he visited Coventry after it was flattened by a German air raid. I thought that Helga better knock off the baby talk or she'll have a company of Royal Marine Commandos show up at her door some afternoon at tea time for a little chat.

"So Helga," I said, "President Truman heard you were going to slaughter and cook another King Ranch size herd of cattle, so he issued emergency visas to all the poor people in China to enter the United States. They're lined up outside our door and down the block waiting for a crack at the leftovers."

"They are? Well maybe we should invite them inside. It's chilly outside," said Ingrid.

"Shut up Ingrid," said Helga to her sister. She then turned her gaze back to me and said smugly, "As my Uncle Ole often said, 'better to prepare too much food than not enough,' and he was a very wise man."

"Did he say that before or after they let him out of the lunatic asylum?" I asked.

"Lunatic asylum?" asked Helga in a state of high dudgeon. "Why, I'll have you know that my uncle Ole was a pillar of the community back in Minot. He didn't drink like a fish and smoke like a train engine like some people I know. He was even a deacon in the Episcopalian Church."

"Oh, well, that explains it. You have to keep an eye on those Episcopalians. Did you know that old King Henry the Eighth, the founder of that denomination, chopped off the heads of his wives right and left and also diddled most of their ladies in waiting to boot." I retorted.

I knew I was getting to Helga because her face had turned a nice purple color, the color you sometimes see in ripe heirloom tomatoes. She was so steamed up she was sputtering and at a loss for words. As I was preparing to deliver another salvo, I suddenly noticed that it was getting very warm in the room. I glanced down the table at my wife and noticed that she was shooting a pair of florescent green Lex Luthor kryptonite death rays out of her eyes that converged on a spot in the middle of my forehead. I was afraid that if she turned up the rheostat any higher I would dissolve into a puddle of goo on my seat, so I shut up.

So we all went back to stuffing food into our mouths for a while and Helga's complexion returned to its usual pasty white. I noticed that all the food on the table within a three foot arc of Helga's chair had disappeared, as if by magic.

"Mama, what did Dr. Richman tell you when you saw him yesterday?" my wife asked Helga.

"He said that the reason I have been gaining so much weight lately could be because of a gland problem. He's going to run some tests," said Helga, as she was shoving a heaping tablespoon full of creamed corn into her pie hole. By my count this was the third doctor she had gone to because she was gaining weight like a force fed goose getting its liver fat enough to make pate. Helga was convinced that she had some mysterious condition making her fatter, but the first two doctors she had seen told her to just stop eating so much.

I opened my mouth to make a sincere and helpful comment, but suddenly I felt the florescent green Lex Luthor kryptonite death rays focused on my forehead again. After that I lost interest in the conversation going on around the table.

By the time the coffee and apple pie was served, all I wanted to do was go in my den, loosen my belt three holes and have some more bourbon. I would need the bourbon to fortify myself for when I caught holy hell for my conduct earlier after my in-laws left.

The telephone started to ring in the foyer. This was odd; we seldom got calls after six in the evening. Besides, most of the people my wife talked with on the phone on a regular basis were there at the dinner party. I didn't jump up and answer it. That was my wife's job. After all, it was her house and I was just graciously allowed to live there under certain specified conditions. Despite what was written on the deed, she owned the place, lock, stock and barrel. I didn't in any way feel like I was lonelier than the Lone Ranger to find myself in this situation, because it was the norm all across the country. Don't believe me? Take even a cursory look at middle class divorce settlements in America in 1950. In 99 percent of the cases, the wife got the house.

June walked into the dining room where Helga and I were engaged in a spirited game of avoiding eye contact with each other. "Matt, it's for you. I think it's something to do with your work," she said.

Work stuff? I wondered what was going on. The only person at my work who knew my home number was Caroline Adderley and she would hesitate to call me at home except under the direst circumstances. I hurried into the foyer and picked up the receiver and put it to my ear. "Hello, this is Matt Cole," I said.

"Ye,s Mr. Cole, my name is Nathan Marx. You don't know me but you employ my daughter Josephine at your detective agency. I called the emergency number posted on the front door of your office and spoke to a woman who gave me your home number. You'll have to forgive me but I'm very upset right now."

"Calm down, Mr. Marx and tell me what'd wrong. Did something happen to your daughter?" I asked.

"Yes, Josephine and a friend named Sam Carter were beaten within an inch of their lives. Sam is in a coma but Josephine is conscious, thank God. They are in Queen of the Angels Hospital. Josephine won't talk to the police. She said she would only talk to you. I need you to come here, Mr. Cole, and talk to her and give me some answers as soon as you can."

'Sit tight, Mr. Marx, I'll be right there," I said, with my mouth set in a hard line.

I was out the door without speaking to anyone, pausing only to pick up my car keys from the table beside the door. Queen of Angels Hospital was on Bellevue Avenue in Echo Park. I made it there in record time, several times going airborne in my Cadillac coming out of dips in the road and treating stop signs as discretionary. When I arrived I parked in a red zone near the main entrance and made my way inside as fast as my game leg would let me. In the main lobby I was met by a man who I assumed was Nathan Marx.

A slim man in his fifties, five nine or ten, with poor posture, he was wearing dark slacks, a brown sweater, an open collared white shirt and had a yarmulke perched on the back of his head. His eyes were large and sad and his face somber. An untucked tail of his shirt poking out from under the sweater gave evidence that he had dressed in a hurry.

"Mr. Marx, I'm Matt Cole," I said, as I hobbled up to the man.

'Thank God," said Marx, and turned on his heel and strode toward a bank of two elevators. I limped after him going as fast as my bad leg would let me. Taking the first elevator to open, we rode it in silence to the third floor and got off. I had the distinct feeling that Marx wasn't too happy with me and I couldn't blame him. If I was in his position I would probably feel the same.

Standing in the doorway of JoJo's hospital room I hesitated before going in. Seeing that lively, spunky girl lying there swathed in bandages with an I.V. connecting her arm to a suspended bottle of liquid was heartbreaking and I felt a sudden surge of guilt wash over me.

The Brat: "Well, here's another innocent you've hurt by your incompetence. You should have sidelined her when you first understood the danger you both were in."

I had no reply because I agreed with him. I approached the bed. JoJo was lying there with her eyes closed. Bandages covered her head and the part of her chest I could see above the hospital blanket. Both her eyes were black and blue and the bridge of her nose was encased in a splint indicating that it had been broken. I noticed that both her hands and lower forearms were also encased in bandages. I was about to speak to her and wake her up as gently as I could when she opened her eyes of her own accord. It took her a moment to focus but then her eyes landed on her father.

"Daddy, go out in the hall. I need to talk to Matt alone," she croaked. Nathen Marx at first seemed to want to protest but then he hung his head and did as she asked. When we were alone, JoJo's eyes drifted back to me.

"Hello, Matt, looks like I've gotten myself in a bit of a jam" she said, and attempted a slight smile.

"Who did this to you JoJo?" I asked.

"It was that cop, Lieutenant Brandywine, and his skinny partner. They also beat up Sam. The nurses tell me he is in a coma and I'm really worried about him."

"How did you run into them? I told you to go see a movie with Sam."

"After I left you at the office I went home. Sam came over because we had a date tonight. When he arrived I got this idea to go back to that councilman's house and question the servants. I figured that rich people are so used to having servants around them that they sometimes forget they're there. I was hoping that one of the servants at Conrad's house might have heard some conversation between the father and the son that would shed light on Daisy's disappearance. I wanted to impress you with my ability to investigate on my own," said JoJo. She asked for a sip of water and I helped her drink from a glass through a glass straw. She then continued.

"Well, we staked the place out in my car and waited until Councilman Conrad left in his big limousine. I rang the doorbell and started talking to the maid who answered the door. After a few questions I really felt we were on to something. She looked like she was struggling with her conscience about something. The maid's name is Doris; she's about fifty, kind of stout with gray hair. I'm positive she was about to tell me something important but I'll never know what because Sam and I were grabbed from behind by some big guys, maybe bodyguards, maybe just the butler and the gardener, I don't know who they were. They locked us in a closet. About thirty minutes later the closet door was opened and there stood Brandywine and his partner. They handcuffed Sam and me behind our backs, took us out to their car and locked us both in the trunk. The car took off and we were on flat ground for a while and then began climbing a grade. I could tell we were traveling uphill because Sam and I rolled against the back of the trunk. After about a half-hour total of driving, the car stopped, the trunk lid opened and we were dragged out. It was almost dark by that time but I could tell we were out of the city in some brushy area," said JoJo. I noticed tears suddenly form in the corners of her eyes and her face contorted in pain.

"Do you want to stop now?" I asked. "You can tell me the rest later."

"No, I have to tell you it all. They hit us with those clubs you see policemen carrying when they walk their beats. Brandywine said to the other cop, 'I'll handle the Jew bitch. You take her boyfriend.' He hurt me Matt. He started off stomping on my hands and then switched to the club. Each time that he hit me he would say something like, 'How's that feel you Jew cunt,' or 'take that you sheeny whore.' After hitting me for a while he leaned in close to me and started talking to me. He said: 'I'm not gonna hit you in the mouth cause I want you to deliver a message to your boss, that gimpy legged PI. Tell him this is happening to you cause he wouldn't obey our orders to stop poking around in things he shouldn't. Tell him that the same thing that's happening to you could also happen to his cute blonde wife and little baby if he don't back off.' A few minutes after that Brandywine hit me in the head and I got knocked out. I woke up on a paved street somewhere with a woman screaming near me."

"Okay, JoJo, that's enough for now. I want you to rest and get well. We'll talk again later," I said.

While I was looking into JoJo's eyes, I saw them change. Instead of the remembered terror I saw in them when she told her story, I saw anger and fury in them now. She reached out a bandaged hand and placed it gently on my arm.

"Matt, I want somebody to pay those bastards back for what they did to Sam and me. Promise me that they'll be paid back."

"Oh, you're gonna get payback for this JoJo. You're gonna get payback in spades," I said, meaning every word.

CHAPTER NINETEEN

BEL AIR
LOS ANGELES
NOVEMBER 25, 1951
9: 30 A.M.

I was sitting in the driver's seat of a parked maroon 1946 Chevrolet coupe I had purchased on Friday from a used car dealer for 350 dollars. The body was a little beat up and it had about an inch of dirt on it, but it ran just fine. The inside was littered with empty Chinese food take out containers, hamburger wrappers and used paper coffee cups. This buying of beat-up old used cars to use as camouflage while investigating cases was getting to be a habit with me. I figured that the way I was going I'd have enough old heaps to open my own used car lot pretty soon. I was watching the street entrance to Councilman Conrad's Bel Air mansion. I wasn't parked on his street, but on a little turnout just wide enough for my car under a live oak tree on a switchback road higher up the ridge. I had picked the spot because it offered a sorta good view of the politician's posh abode through binoculars, and an unobstructed view of the entrance to his driveway.

From seven in the morning until dark all day Friday and Saturday I had occupied the same spot. On Saturday a police car with two uniformed cops inside had stopped to check me out. I showed them my driver's license and my P.I. license and told them I was investigating a wayward husband. One of the cops filled out a three by five inch field interrogation card with my information and then they drove away and left me alone. It was Sunday morning now and I hoped that my target would appear soon, I was getting tired of sitting and my back hurt from the worn out seat of the Chevy.

§

On Thursday night when I limped out of JoJo's hospital room I was angry and frustrated. I thought about calling Lt. Miller in Chief Parker's office and asking him to pick up Brandywine and Connors and book them for attempted murder. But almost immediately I dismissed the notion. By this time both of those skunks would have lined up four or five witnesses who would testify that the two cops were drinking in a bar or out dancing with friends or some such at the time of JoJo's and Sam's assault, giving them an air tight alibi. No, this would be have to be handled in a different way, the law of the jungle way. But what concerned me most right then was the conversation I had to have with Nathan Marx and I dreaded it.

"Your daughter and her friend were beaten up by someone connected to a case she and I were investigating. I tried to remove her from the case when it got dangerous, but JoJo begged me not to and she can be very persuasive. Still, I take full responsibility for what happened to her. I don't blame you for being angry with me," I said to him in the hospital hallway.

"That's where you're wrong Mr. Cole. I'm not angry at you. I'm angry at the men who could do such a thing to these two young people. I know my daughter; I know how persuasive she can be. Since she was a little girl she has rebelled when someone, anyone told her she couldn't do something or conversely ordered her to do something. She used to give my poor wife fits before she died. If I, her father, am not able to influence her, I have no right to expect you as her employer to be able to. I just want you to give me your word that the people who did this horrible thing will be brought to justice."

"Mr. Marx, you have my word. The people who did this will pay dearly, very dearly, or I'll die trying," I answered.

An older man in a white coat turned a corner, saw Marx and me talking and joined us. "I'm Dr. Jenkins, are you a policeman?" he asked.

"No, just a friend of Miss Marx. How is she?"

"Well, aside from a broken leg, broken arm, dislocated shoulder, smashed hands, three broken ribs, a concussion and contusions all over her body, she's doing fine. I sincerely hope that the police find and punish the animals that did this to her," said the doctor.

"Yeah, me too," I replied. I wanted to ask the doctor what he would suggest be done, when in this instance, the animals he wanted punished by the police, were policemen themselves.

When I got home I discovered that all my in-laws had gone home and was relieved. June asked me where I went in such a hurry. I gave her a bullshit cover story but I knew she was aware I was lying. We went to bed and I slept fitfully, waking repeatedly. Sometime in the middle of the night I had to rise and down a couple of shots of bourbon in order to go back to sleep. I slouched into the lobby of my office just after it opened, a little after eight. Betty, the receptionist stopped me.

"Mr. Cole, there's a gentleman here to see you. He arrived a few moments before you did," she said

I turned toward the waiting area and saw a man rising from one of the chairs. He was in his mid-thirties wearing a blue blazer, tan slacks and an open necked shirt. He appeared athletic but had long tennis player muscles rather than the knotty working man's type. He also sported a full head of wavy brown hair worn longer than most men. But what drew my attention the most was his insolent air and the smirk he wore on his handsome face.

"You want to talk to me," I asked, calling it across the room.

"Yes, Cole, there are some things we need to discuss. I'm Mike Conrad."

Holding my temper, although it was hard, I told him to follow me to my private office. Once inside, I sat down behind my desk and Conrad sat opposite me. Before speaking he produced a gold cigarette case, took out a butt and lit it with a gold lighter, the very picture of nonchalance. Then he reached into his breast pocket and his hand came out clutching a fat legal sized envelope which he tossed on the desk in front of me.

"There's ten thousand dollars in that envelope and it's yours if you drop this miserable little inquiry into the death of a whore named Rhonda Faye," he said, still smirking. I found myself wishing the smooth bastard would give me an excuse to smash his face in.

"That's peculiar," I replied, "I don't remember telling anyone that I thought Rhonda Faye was dead. Are you admitting to me now that you choked her to death during a bout of rough sex and then had the body disposed of like a piece of trash? You see, I found Rhonda's john book. There's a page in it that tells all about your sexual preferences." The smirk disappeared from his face and was replaced by a fierce glare.

"I'm not admitting anything. You have no proof that I had anything to do with her disappearance or death or whatever. What I want to know is why you're making such a fuss over a whore. They're a dime a dozen and nobody else gives a shit about them in this city."

"Well, I care, and I'm gonna keep digging until I find evidence that you killed that girl. It's out there somewhere just waiting to be found. I want to see the look on your upper class effete face when a judge sends you away for a long stretch in the gray bar hotel for what you've done," I answered as I threw the fat envelope back into his lap, stood and walked around the desk. Conrad also stood and glared at me.

"You'll be sorry for not being reasonable," he said, through gritted teeth.

"I think it's time for you to leave," I said, with a smirk of my own.

We were standing face to face, about a foot apart; Conrad suddenly made a grab for the knot of my tie with his left hand while cocking back his right arm preparing to sock me. I whipped up my good right leg and my knee smashed like a jackhammer into his balls. He doubled over and deflated like the South Sea Bubble. I grabbed a fistful of the front of his silk shirt and gave him an old fashioned uppercut to the jaw like Hoot Gibson invariably uses to knock out the black hatted rustlers in his movies. I then proceeded to bitch slap Conrad all over my office. I was pretty steamed so I don't remember how long I slapped him around. It was probably somewhere between a few seconds and a minute. By the time I was through, he was dazed, disoriented and had fiery red cheeks. He looked like he was ready to pass out on me. I dragged him out of my private door that opened onto a straight hallway that led to the rear stairwell of the building. At the top of the stairs I slammed his back against a wall.

"Don't get any fancy ideas about calling the cops and having me arrested. By the time the cops arrive I'll have five witnesses lined up who'll testify that you stormed in here and tried to assault me. Then I'll visit a reporter with the Times I know and start singing about an entitled, rich, murdering snob and a woman he used and abused and who wound up dead and just like that your daddy will never be Lieutenant Governor," I whispered in his ear. I then threw his ass down the stairs.

Back in my office, I picked up the phone and called Chief Parker's office in city hall and asked for Lt. Miller.

"This is Miller."

"Yeah, Matt Cole here, remember you told me that you were going to provide protection for my family? I just want to verify that you followed through on that."

"As we speak, at least two heavily armed members of the LAPD. Gangster Squad are watching your house front and back around the clock. Your family is as safe as they would be in church," replied Miller. I thanked him and hung up.

I buzzed Betty on the intercom and asked her to tell Caroline Adderley to step into my office. When my office manager entered she appeared concerned. "How is Miss Marx? I received a call last night from her father. He said she was beaten up. How did it happen," she asked.

"She's in Queen of the Angels Hospital. I don't know her condition today. Maybe you could visit her later and see if we as an organization can do anything for her while she is recovering. But what I really called you in here for is to tell you that I'm going to be out of the office for a few days." I said.

"You're going after the people that beat her up, aren't you? You should let the police handle it,"

"No Caroline, I want to handle this myself. There are some things that are personal."

Before leaving my office, I opened my safe and retrieved Daisy's john book and flipped through it one more time. I had never met her but I felt I knew her all the same. I put the red book back in the safe. Next, I took an item from the safe and replaced it with a similar item, grabbed a thousand dollars in cash, closed the door and spun the dial. Then I had a thought and opened the safe again. I took a Smith & Wesson, .38 caliber, Chief's special revolver from a shelf. It was my back up weapon. I didn't carry it much because carrying one gun was enough of a pain in the ass in itself. But with all that had happened recently, I felt I might need another gun if things got dicey. Switching off the light as I left, I made my way home.

When I came in the front door of my house, June looked up from reading the morning paper. "Why are you home so soon?" she asked.

I sat her down on the sofa and told her all about my investigation into the disappearance of Daisy Carter and also about the beating of JoJo. "Why, that poor girl, and the other woman, too. She didn't deserve that, even if she was a prostitute." she said, when I finished. "Bastards like that should be gelded, both the rich playboy and those two cops."

I put my arms around her and told her I was going underground for a few days. She gazed into my eyes for a moment, then said, "Do what you have to do." I was so overcome with love for her. I felt like I was batting 1000 with the women I had chosen to be around me in my life. I packed a small bag, called a cab and had the cabbie drive me to the intersection of Alameda and 6th Street where he let me out. I made my way a couple of blocks north to a used car lot where I bought my Chevy. For a couple of days I staked out the Conrad mansion during the day and slept in a rundown motel by night.

§

A little after ten o'clock in the morning I spotted an old pickup truck descending the driveway of the Conrad mansion. With the naked eye I could see that there were two people in it but no details. I quickly brought the binoculars to my eyes and after a little searching, the truck loomed large in the eyepieces. The driver was an older man with a mustache, wearing a blue coat with a tie. The passenger was a woman in her fifties with gray hair. I recognized her as the maid, Doris, who had shown JoJo and I out the door when we were kicked out by Councilman Conrad.

I started up my Chevy and accelerated around a hairpin turn and down the hill in time to fall in behind the pickup truck. The driver of the truck was driving a sedate 25 M.P.H. and wasn't attempting any evasive maneuvers so I held back and increased the distance between us. The truck's driver remained five miles under the speed limit and carefully followed all the traffic laws all the way to his destination.

After about twenty-five minutes or so of driving, the pickup pulled into a parking lot on the west side of a little Baptist Church at the intersection of Bundy and Santa Monica Boulevard in the Sawtelle area. I parked in a spot that had a good view of the front entrance to the church and saw Doris, carrying a bible and accompanied by her male companion, walk in the door close behind another couple. I looked at the church sign and saw that the Sunday service time was 11a.m. I glanced at my watch. It was 10: 55.

My stomach was grumbling and in need of food, and I knew I had a whole hour to go before Doris emerged from the church. I considered whether to find a local diner or coffee shop and get something to eat. In the end I decided not to chance it. If for some reason the church let out early I might miss the opportunity to talk to Doris the maid and I didn't know when I would get another chance. So I compensated for my hunger by chain smoking Lucky Strikes and drinking cold coffee from a paper cup. The time passed slowly.

At 12 noon on the dot people started to emerge from the church, each one stopping to shake the hand of the pastor on the church's front step.

The Brat: "Now that's the kind of preacher I like, one who will stick to a schedule. We could have got one of those guys that gets all would up in his sermon and loses track of time. We could have been waiting here all afternoon."

When Doris and her male companion emerged from the church door, I bailed out of the Chevy and approached her on a walkway that stretched across a patch of grass. "Excuse me, Ma'am. My name is Matthew Cole," I said, as I tugged at the brim of my fedora.

"Yes, I know who you are. I recognize you from when you were at the house the other day," she said, looking at me with apprehension.

"Doris, who is this man?" asked her gentleman friend. Up close I could see that his blue suit was shiny at the elbows and frayed at the cuffs.

"Mr. Cole, this is my husband Frank. He's one of the gardeners at the Conrad estate." We greeted each other and shook hands. Then to her husband, Doris said, "Frank, go on to the car. I'll be there in just a minute." Frank reluctantly complied with his wife's wishes.

"I'm here bothering you on your Sunday because my assistant, Miss Marx, told me she thought you might have information about a missing woman," I said, as diplomatically as I knew how.

Doris bit her lip for a moment and then spoke. "You know, I've been struggling with my conscience about what I saw and heard for over a month. I finally decided to keep quiet so as not to jeopardize my and my husband's positions at the estate. But a while ago I was listening to the pastor's sermon. He was talking about lying. About how there are different kinds of lies. He said that not speaking up when we witness evil can be a form of lying. He then reminded us that Jesus never lied." Doris said while clutching her bible to her chest.

"So, I'm going to tell you what I saw and if it means Frank and I lose our jobs, so be it. I feel now that it's my duty as a Christian to reveal what I know. A little over a month ago on a Saturday night way after midnight, I was hanging around the kitchen. The councilman often stayed up late reading in his study. I couldn't go to bed before he did because he might ring for some warm milk or something and if I wasn't there I could get in trouble. There was suddenly a pounding on the front door and I ran to answer it. I looked through the peep hole and saw that it was the councilman's son outside the door. I had no sooner thrown the bolt when Mike Conrad, all excited and mussed up brushed past me and rushed into his father's study. I couldn't tell whether he was drunk or just hysterical. I went and stood beside the study door out of sight to hear what was said. I shouldn't have done it but I was curious and wanted to be near in case they needed me for something."

'Then the councilman's son blurted out, 'Dad, I'm in a jam. I think I just killed a woman, a prostitute. She's still up at my house naked in my bed. Dad, she won't wake up.' 'What makes you think you killed her?' asked the councilman. 'Because I choked her. I think I choked her too long,' he said. 'Alright, I'll deal with it. Let me make some calls.' said the councilman. After that the door was slammed and I didn't hear anything more. That's all I know," said Doris.

"Thank you, Doris. I appreciate the courage it must have taken for you to tell me this."

"Will I have to go to court and testify?" she asked.

'I don't know, possibly," I replied.

"God's will be done," said Doris, and then went to join her husband in the pickup truck. As I watched her walk away I was heartened. As cynical as I was, it was good to know that there were still people out there who at great personal risk, were willing to do what was morally right.

The first thing I did after speaking to Doris the maid was to find a diner to sate my hunger. A block away from the Baptist church I saw one on the west side of Santa Monica Boulevard and parked on the street in front. It was called 'Friendly's Diner" and it appeared to be filling up fast with the people just out of church. I was lucky enough to snag a stool at the counter and ordered two ham sandwiches on rye and coffee. After eating I felt refreshed.

I'm sure the three cups of coffee had something to do with that. I paid the bill of $1.89, and left a fifty cent tip.

On the way out of the diner I spied a pay phone bolted to the wall by the front door with a thick phone book hanging from it by a chain. After looking up the number in the phone book, I called Queen of the Angels Hospital. When the switchboard operator answered, I asked for the nurse in ward three.

"Ward three, this is Sister Patricia. How may I help you?"

"Yes, I'm a family friend. I was wondering how Miss Marx is faring," I said into the phone receiver.

"She's doing well. The pain is subsiding and she has begun to eat. That's always a good sign," replied Sister Patricia.

"How about Sam Carter? He's also a patient there" I said.

"I'm so sorry but Samuel Carter died early this morning from his injuries."

CHAPTER TWENTY

SAWTELLE AREA
LOS ANGELES
NOVEMBER 25, 1951
1: 30 P.M.

When I first became a rookie L.A.P.D. cop in 1936, I was assigned to a radio car with a seasoned officer named Grinnell. Being at least thirty pounds overweight, the other cops had given Grinnell the nickname of "Porky." Because of the endless parade of victims we dealt with on a nightly basis I began to hate and despise strong arm robbers, rapists, hugger muggers, thieves and even small time criminals like pickpockets for the harm they inflicted upon the most vulnerable members of society.

One night, after I had just broken the nose of a wife beater, "Porky" Grinnell pulled me aside and gave me some advice. "You're gonna have to wind it down a notch kid. At the rate you're going you'll burn out in six months tops. Don't hate these assholes. Think of them as a herd of cattle and we're cowboys driving them up from Texas to the railhead at Abilene. The ones that stray away from the others and do bad things we either shoot on the spot or just drive them back to their place in the herd. Don't hate them because it will hurt you more than them." As I got more experience as a policeman, I came to appreciate the wisdom of Porky's advice. Becoming emotionally involved with people on the street was a no-no.

Well, when I stepped out of that diner on Santa Monica Boulevard, I was violating all my long held, self-enforced rules. I had become emotionally involved. I hated Lt. Brandywine and his pal, Sgt. Connors. It wasn't a sudden fierce flare-up of hate that often passes with time. This hate was the kind that is cold and calculating and just sits down there in your gut and festers.

I spent the afternoon driving around the downtown area looking for a suitable location to do what I had in mind. At around four p.m. I found what I was looking for on Santa Fe Avenue just north of 6th Street. It was an abandoned factory that backed up to railroad tracks and beyond that the L.A. River. I parked in front of the rundown building and made my way up to its big, dilapidated, weathered wood front swinging doors. They weren't locked so I swung one of the tall doors open enough to get through and entered the building.

I was a long rectangular room with a stained concrete floor and pools of oil here and there. Light flooded in from skylights on the ceiling. The first thing that caught my eye was a huge pile of wooden packing boxes piled up in the center of the room. It looked like whoever packed up the machinery that once stood here had brought too many boxes with him and just left them here in a pile rather than taking the trouble to haul them out again. To my left I saw a wooden stairway that led up to a glassed in office that overlooked the factory floor. The windows of the office were smeared, dusty and almost opaque. I climbed the stairs to the office. In a drawer of a broken desk I found some papers that indicated that the company that had last occupied the building was called the K.L. Houghton Co. and they manufactured aluminum canteens and canteen cups for the government between early 1943 and mid-1945. I looked through the dirty window at the factory floor. I could imagine rows of machines stamping out aluminum canteen halves and workers in another area busily joining the sides together with arc welders. Then suddenly the huge mound of packing crates on the factory floor gave me an idea. Instead of what I had intended to do in my upcoming encounter with the two crooked cops, I decided that something a little more creative might work better. The more I thought about my idea, the more I figured it might just work.

After descending the stairs to the factory floor I took off my suit jacket and hat and set about arranging packing crates from the pile in rows and stacks blocking off the back half of the floor. It took me a long time because I was careful to make the placement of the crates look jumbled and haphazard and not staged. The only way past the obstruction was a narrow walkway through the center of the crates that ended in a cul-de-sac about twenty feet in.

Standing back, I surveyed my work and was satisfied. I put my jacket and fedora back on and limped out the front doors. I propped both the big doors open with two discarded cinder blocks I found nearby and drove away west on 6th Street into the sunset.

At 6:30, I stopped at a phone booth on Alameda and called the phone number listed for the Conrad mansion. A male voice answered.

"Councilman Conrad's residence, this is the butler speaking."

"I need to speak to the councilman. My name is Matthew Cole and I'm a private investigator. If he instructs you to hang up on me, tell him that it wouldn't be in his best interests to do so because I've uncovered enough evidence to send his son to prison for about twenty years," I said.

"Just a moment, sir," replied the butler. I heard the sound of the telephone receiver being laid down on a table. I waited about two minutes before the senior Conrad picked up the phone.

"What do you want Cole?" asked the elder Conrad gruffly..

"I want you to meet me one hour from now at a vacant lot on the northeast corner of Alameda and 7th Street. Come alone. I want to discuss some evidence I've uncovered that implicates your son in the murder of Doris Carter. Maybe we can make a deal."

There was a few moments pause and then the councilman answered. "Alright, I'll be there"

I killed the hour wait sitting in a downtown diner drinking coffee and chain smoking Lucky Strikes. I rehearsed in my mind the moves I would have to make later. I had to admit to myself that there was very little margin for error. I would have to perform perfectly or I would end up dead.

I timed it so I got to the intersection of 7th Street and Alameda Avenue at 7:30 on the dot. I saw that Councilman Conrad had beaten me there. I saw him standing beside a little red MG sport's car in the vacant lot on the northeast corner. I pulled into the lot and parked my Chevy beside the MG and got out.

I didn't greet Conrad or thank him for coming or any of that horseshit. I just came right out with what I had to say. 'I've got solid evidence, enough to convict in superior court, that your asshole son strangled to death a call girl named Daisy Carter on the night of October 21, 1951 while the two were engaged in a sex act at his house in Laurel Canyon. The evidence is solid enough to support a conviction for involuntary manslaughter, maybe even murder two because the body was disposed of. I also have evidence that your son came to you after the killing and told you about it. You helped him cover the whole thing up. That makes you an accessory. And in California law, an accessory to a crime is as guilty as a principal."

"You make me out to be a monster, but I'm not," said Councilman Conrad. "My only son came to me in trouble and I helped him cover up a mistake, but I didn't intend to break the law. I was just blinded by my love for my only son. I feel sorrow for that poor woman even though she was a prostitute. And I've been paid back for my mistake many times since. That night when Mike came to me and told me what he had done, I called my political assistant Jack. He got in touch with one of Jack Dragna's hoodlums without my knowledge. Dragna's men disposed of the woman's body but I don't know where. Since then I have been Dragna's man on the council. He tells me how to vote on almost every issue."

"If you're looking to me for sympathy, save your breath. A month ago there were two surviving members of the Carter family in Los Angeles, Daisy and Sam Carter. They were just ordinary people, not famous or rich like you, and now they're both dead thanks to the actions of your pampered son," I said, my voice dripping with contempt.

"You mentioned a deal when we spoke on the phone," replied Conrad.

"Yeah, the deal is this: Go to the district attorney, I'm sure the two of you are old pals and golfing buddies, and fess up to this crime within twenty-four hours. If you don't, I'm taking my evidence to the D.A. myself after I lay it all out for the newspapers."

Conrad didn't say anything more. He just nodded, got in his little sport's car and drove away east on 7th Street. I got in my Chevy and started the motor. I pulled out of the vacant lot and drove north on Alameda keeping an eye on my rear view mirror. After about half a block I saw a pair of headlights snap on behind me just as I knew they would. In the dim light from the streetlamps I could see it was a black 1950 Ford. Under the light from the streetlamps it appeared to be dark green, but I knew it was black. As I was making a right turn to go eastbound on 6th Street, a red light suddenly appeared in the passenger side windshield of the Ford. After completing my turn, instead of pulling over, I mashed the gas pedal of my Chevy to the floor and took off with a roar.

I had deliberately chosen my meeting site with Conrad to be close to the abandoned factory that was my ultimate destination. This was to keep Brandywine and Connors from being able to radio for help. The last thing I needed at the time was for a bunch of uniformed cops to show up and complicate matters. My sudden acceleration must have caught the crooked cops by surprise because I was able to open up a half block lead on them. I roared east on 6th Street using every last horsepower available in the Chevy's inline six. I made a sliding left turn onto Santa Fe, then almost immediately a right into the driveway of the abandoned factory. Sliding to a stop in the dirt next to the door, I immediately abandoned my car and ducked inside the factory. Crossing the front part of the factory floor using my trademark "wounded antelope" gait because of my crippled left leg, I was approaching the entrance to the walkway between the crates when the police ford came barreling through the door and Connors hit the brakes hard. A patch of oil on the floor caused the police car to slew a little to the left and come to a stop about six feet from the packing cases. Both cops jumped out and ran to positions on either side of the narrow opening in the cases. By this time, I was ten feet in and still running but I could see that I was running out of room. The dead end in the aisle was just ahead.

"You can stop running, buddy boy, you got nowhere to go," said Brandywine. I stopped.

"Now you can turn around slowly and take your gun out and throw it away and raise your hands," said Connors. I turned and took my .38 backup revolver from my coat pocket and tossed it away. But I complied with his last instruction only partly. Instead of raising my hands, I held my arms out extended from my sides. Brandywine and Connors were standing there smiling, each with a .38 revolver in hand pointed at me.

"Okay, asshole, we want that whore's john book and everything else you've collected about her case," said Brandywine insolently. "And if you're stubborn and don't lead us to where it is, we'll pay a visit to that pretty little blonde wife of yours and show her what a real man feels like inside her. We might even see if that little baby of yours will float in one of those scummy pools in the L.A. River.."

"Walk toward us slowly or we'll shoot you," commanded Connors.

I shook my head. "If you shoot me, you'll never find the john book. I've made arrangements to have it and all my other evidence sent to the D.A. if I disappear suddenly,"

"Hells bells," said Brandywine. "We'll just have to come in there and get you, but it's gonna mean some extra pain for you later on." He walked into the pathway with his gun still in his hand, followed by Connors about ten feet behind him.

People I deal with in my line of work are always underestimating me. They think that just because I have this game leg and have to hobble around that I will be a pushover in a physical fight. What they don't realize is that I was a street cop for several years and learned how to defend myself well. I also was a combat Marine, having fought tough, fanatical Japanese soldiers hand to hand on more than one occasion. Those brave, incredibly dedicated Japanese I had bested would have had Brandywine and Connors for breakfast.

When Brandywine was about four feet from me, thinking that I was unarmed, he holstered his revolver and reached in a coat pocket for his handcuffs. What he didn't realize was that because of the narrow walkway, the bulk of his body was shielding me from his partner's gun. It was a stupid, rookie mistake but I'm sure it was done out of hubris. These guys were probably used to getting by with shit like that all the time and no one held them to account because they were cops.

My right hand flashed to the small of my back. I grabbed the butt of my Colt Government Model pistol, pulled it out of its holster, whipped it through the air and brought the slide down hard across the bridge of Brandywine's big, blue veined nose. The crooked cop's ugly smeller exploded in a cloud of blood and cartilage, stunning him. Both of the big man's hands flew to his face and he bent forward at the waist. I squatted down, keeping Brandywine's body between me and the muzzle of Connor's gun. I sighted my pistol along the Lieutenant's back as I heard the sound of the soles of Conner's shoes pounding toward me on the concrete floor. When his head came into view over Brandywine's back I fired, the sound of the shot echoing in the empty factory.

The military surplus, "hardball," .45 caliber bullet hit Connors dead center in his upper lip, about midway between his mouth and the base of his nose. I saw a red mist appear behind his head like a grotesque halo as the bullet struck. Connors stumbled to a stop, staring straight ahead, but he didn't fall right away. He blinked his eyes several times looking at me in surprise and then finally, he fell straight back. His heels drummed on the concrete floor for a second or two and then he was still.

I stood up and went forward to relieve Brandywine of the pistol in his shoulder holster. Then I backed a few feet away from him, still keeping him covered with my pistol. The lieutenant had recovered sufficiently by this time that his hands came away from his bloody face and he used them to get shakily to his feet. He looked down at the body of his partner.

"Oh, my God, do you know what you've done? You've killed a cop. Do you know what they do to people who kill cops in this town? It's a one way trip to the gas chamber," said Brandywine. His speech was a little distorted because of his broken nose.

I stepped back a few steps, reached down and picked up an old worn out seat cushion from a packing crate. I had found it upstairs in the office earlier in the afternoon. Then I walked back to the crooked cop.

"Did you imagine I would let you two keep breathing and walking around on the earth after you beat up those kids and killed one?" I asked.

"It was Reed's idea. He told us to send a message. I didn't want to do it. What are you doing?"

While he was talking I brought the old seat cushion up in front of me with my left hand and pushed the muzzle of the pistol into it with my right while still keeping it aimed at Brandywine.

"Do you know what the average person thinks when he hears the sound of a gunshot? First he's alarmed, but then in a little while he begins to question if it really was a gunshot or not. When he doesn't hear another shot, he generally passes it off as a backfiring car or somebody dropping something heavy onto a hard surface. But if he hears more than one gunshot, he will usually call the police. Oh, and by the way, if I get the gas chamber for killing one cop, what will they give me for killing two? Will they gas me twice?" I asked.

"Don't do it!" said Brandywine hysterically.

"This is for JoJo Marx and Sam Carter," I said and fired through the seat cushion, prompting a small cloud of feathers to blow out the other side. It was hard to aim with the cushion in the way, but I did pretty well. The bullet caught Brandywine just below the left eye. The sound of the shot had been well muted by the cushion. It wasn't much louder than a book being slammed down on a desk.

I left the bodies where they lay. I didn't touch the police car either but left it idling where it sat. Earlier in the day I had been careful to wipe my fingerprints off of any hard surfaces I had touched inside the factory. Since I hadn't touched anything this trip, I was in the clear. I did pick up the two .45 caliber shell casings and my backup pistol and put those items in my jacket pocket where they nestled beside Brandywine's gun. I didn't worry about the footprints of my shoes in the dust on the concrete floor. I wore size eleven Florsheim lace ups in a style that the company had sold about a gazillion pairs of all around the state. Tracing them was impossible but just to be on the safe side, I would get rid of them when I returned home. That done, I took one last look around inside the factory and left the building. I moved my car off the dirt beside the door and parked it with the engine running on the street. I went back and rubbed out my car's tire tracks in the dirt beside the door with my shoe, got in my Chevy and drove away.

Captain Straight: "I'm still trying to wrap my head around the fact that you just killed two cops."

The Brat: "Bullshit. Those two assholes quit being cops years ago. What Matt just did was the same as a farmer shooting two rats running along a fence line with a .22 rifle.

§

In 1943 when I came home from the war and opened my private investigation business I had to get a permit to carry a concealed pistol from the Los Angeles Sheriff's Department. One of the questions on the form I had to fill out asked for the make, model and serial number of the pistol I would be carrying around. I listed my Colt Government Model pistol in .38 Super caliber, that I had just bought at Sears & Roebuck and Co. That pistol was now safely locked in my safe at my office.

The other Colt Government Model Pistol I had just used for rodent control was one I purchased a couple of years back at a pawn shop in San Pedro for forty bucks cash and no questions asked. It had checkered walnut grips and a military parkerized finish on its metal parts and was marked "PROPERTY OF U. S. ARMY" on the slide. It came with a box of surplus military ammo as a bonus. I had switched the two pistols the day after JoJo was beaten up.

At nine o'clock I pulled my Chevrolet off Highway 1 and followed a rutted road to a bluff overlooking a beach about half way between L.A. and Malibu. I took out the .45 pistol and quickly field stripped it into its component parts. One by one I threw the parts as well as the two shell casings as far out into the Pacific Ocean as I could. That done I took out Brandywine's revolver and also sent it sailing out into the pacific. In a few days the guns would begin to rust. In six months they would be only rusted hunks of unrecognized metal resting on the ocean floor.

CHAPTER TWENTY-ONE

FAIRFAX DISTRICT
LOS ANGELES
NOVEMBER 26, 1951
8:45 A.M.

"Aw c'mon, sugar, not any more," I said as June placed two more pancakes on my plate with a spatula. "If you keep this up I'm going to weigh six hundred pounds and be trapped in here. I won't be able to get out of the door."

"You need your nourishment, after all breakfast is the most important meal of the day," she replied.

"If you say that Uncle Ole often said that I'm going to divorce you."

I was sitting at the kitchen table with Winston sitting across from me in his highchair. His fat little cheeks were smeared with cereal and he was showing the world his usual frown. Then, without any warning at all, Winston's face broke out in a wide toothless grin. It was if he was in possession of some secret knowledge such as, I had forgotten to zip up my fly and Little Matt was hanging out there for everyone in the world to see. It was moments like this that confirmed to me what a lucky man I was.

I had returned home a little after ten the night before. After a shower I fell into bed and slept like a dead man for eight solid hours. When I woke up I enjoyed a leisurely hour's worth of sex with my beautiful wife. It was a good start in getting my life back to normal after the hectic past week.

On the way to my office I stopped and bought a copy of the morning Herald Examiner. As soon as I was alone in my private office, I fired up a Lucky Strike and spread the newspaper out on top of my desk. The banner headline across the top of page one read: "TWO POLICEMEN FOUND SLAIN IN ABANDONED L.A. FACTORY." I skimmed through the story below the headline. It related that two uniformed police officers had seen the open door of the factory at two a.m. while patrolling their beat and went to investigate. They found Lt. Alexander Brandywine and Sgt. Edward Connors, both assigned to the vice division, sprawled on the floor of the warehouse shot dead. A police spokesman declined to comment further, but a confidential source within the police department told a Herald Examiner reporter that authorities believed the slaying was connected to organized crime.

A little further down the page was another, smaller headline that read: "TURMOIL AT CITY HALL." The article below the headline said that the district attorney had called a press conference for eleven o'clock, PDT. Several sources within city hall were relating that it concerned the arrest early that morning of the son of Councilman Michael Conrad on an unspecified charge.

I sat back, snubbed out my cigarette in the ashtray near my right hand, and made the call I had been dreading all morning. I dialed the number Carlo the mountain-and-a-half had given me when he hired me that night at the Olympic Auditorium. He answered me on the fourth ring and we arranged to meet in an hour at Tom Bergin's Public House on Fairfax.

When I entered the bar a few minutes early, I saw Carlo's huge bulk siting at a table in the back. He was wearing a tan sport coat, blue slacks and a white open collared shirt. I sat down across from him and ordered coffee when the waitress came around. Carlo ordered a glass of water.

"I guess there is no easy way to tell you this. Daisy Carter is dead," I said. Carlo's eyes got wild and I thought for a moment that he was going to go berserk and trash the bar. But he settled down and once again looked me in the eye.

"How?" he asked.

"Daisy was working as a high class call girl out of the Havana Club." I thought there would be a reaction from the huge man but all he did was nod.

"So you knew when you hired me what she was?" I asked.

"Yeah, I knew it," replied Carlo. "Do you take me for a fool? Of course I knew she was a call girl. I checked her out a week after I met her. But it didn't matter to me. Daisy did what she had to do to survive. And besides, look at me, when I was working in the rackets for Ben Siegel and Mickey Cohen they would give me orders to beat up and even kill guys, and I did it without mercy. How am I any better than her? How did she die?" Carlo asked, his face a mask of anguish.

"She had a client, Michael Conrad Jr. the son of a Los Angeles city councilman. The sick fuck likes to choke women he's in bed with to heighten his sexual pleasure. Unfortunately for Daisy, he choked her too long the last time. If it's any conciliation to you, the district attorney is going to announce Conrad's indictment for Daisy's killing later this morning. At least, I could do that much for you."

Carlo stared off into space for at least a minute. Then his eyes met mine again. "Okay, Peeper, what do I owe you?"

"Forget it," I answered, "I got enough money. Just call it a favor for an old friend. Oh, by the way, did Daisy ever mention to you anything about a home for girls in Santa Barbara?" I asked.

Carlo shook his head and got up to leave. So Daisy hadn't told Carlo about having a kid stashed away in Santa Barbara. I wasn't about to criticize her. Maybe she was just waiting for an opportune time to tell him.

No sooner had I sat down in the chair in my office than I got a call from Lt. Miller in Chief Parker's office. "My friend needs to meet you at noon in the same place in Chinatown," said Miller.

So I drove to Chinatown to the same Chinese restaurant I visited before, went to the same private room as before and talked to the same Chief Parker sitting at the same table as before.

"I'm sorry I wasn't able to get an incriminating recording of Captain Reed like you wanted me to,' I said.

"It turned out that we didn't need a recording," began Chief Parker. "Your idea to use the rumor mill to tell Dragna that Captain Reed was offering to switch his allegiance to Mickey Cohen worked better than we could ever have imagined. When Reed heard that his enforcers, those two crooked cops Brandywine and Connors, were killed by the Dragna gang last night, he was apparently scared out of his wits. This morning at eight sharp, he put in for his retirement and disappeared. No one can find him. I want to personally thank you for your help in this matter."

"Glad to be of service, chief, but I'm still on Dragna's shit list. He tried to kill me after all," I replied.

"Yes, well, I was coming to that subject. This afternoon I'm going to send Lt. Miller here to meet with Jack Dragna and deliver a message. The message will be that I consider Cohen a bigger threat to the people of Los Angeles than Dragna is. However, if one more attempt is made on the life of you or anyone connected with you, I will come down on him like a ton of bricks and shut down his operations. I will continue the protection of your family until I'm sure that Dragna understands my message. You should be in the clear within the day."

"Thanks Chief," I said and started to rise.

"One last thing." said Parker. "I would appreciate it if our little collaboration in ridding the city of Captain Reed were to remain confidential. Some of the tactics we used might be considered by some as controversial."

"I'll keep quiet for two small favors," I answered. Parker's eyebrows rose and his eyes became hard and wary. "The first concerns a high class call girl ring being run out of the Havana Club on Sunset Boulevard by the manager, Duke Gallagher. I want you to have your new captain in the vice division raid the place and stop it. The second favor is personal. A young woman who works for me has been trying to get hired as a Los Angeles policewoman. She hasn't been able to get to first base because the sergeant receiving the applications is a probably an anti-Semite and keeps blowing her off. I don't demand that you hire her; just give her a fair shot at the job."

For the first time during our talk, Chief Parker smiled. "I think both those things can be arranged," he said.

On the way back to my office I stopped off at Queen of the Angels Hospital to visit JoJo. When I entered her room she was sitting up in bed chatting with one of the ward sisters. When she saw me she smiled. Although still encased in bandages and with a cast on her left arm she appeared alert with lively eyes. I asked her how she was feeling.

"Right now not so good. Have you ever worn a cast? My arm is itching like the devil but I can't scratch it."

"I was sorry to hear about Sam," I said. JoJo's face became sad and she lowered her eyes.

"He was a really nice guy and I feel really guilty about what happened to him. I feel that if I hadn't foolishly dragged him along with me to the Conrad mansion that day, he would still be alive."

"Welcome to the club, I've been getting innocent people hurt and killed with my poor judgement for years. The guilt doesn't go away, but you learn to live with it. Sometimes you make decisions that end up hurting people without intending to." I answered.

JoJo reached out her right hand and placed it on my arm. "Matt I want to thank you. My father told me that you're going to pay my medical bills and my salary while I recuperate. I have to say that for a man, that is a decent thing for you to do."

'Oh, that, I'm just protecting my investment. It's purely a business decision on my part. I can't have it said around town that I don't take care of my employees." I said.

"Oh, now I understand, it was a business decision," replied JoJo wryly.

"Say, young lady, I spoke to some contacts in the police department. I kind of fixed it that when you apply to be a policewoman next time that you will get a fair shot at the job," I said.

"I appreciate your efforts but if it's all the same to you I would like to keep the job I have. I want to continue working for you."

"Are you sure?' I asked. "Being on the police force is way better than spying on wayward husbands and wives for a living."

"There you go. When are you men going to stop trying to make women's decisions for them? This is the twentieth century not the eighteenth. I'm a big girl and I will decide what's good for me. I'm going to continue working for you until you fire me," she replied, but her forceful words were betrayed by the smile on her face.

"Well, you could just quit," I offered.

"Never!"

§

Far away on the east coast in places like New York and Boston, I knew the weather was probably snowy and icy, with people going around in overcoats and carrying umbrellas. But along the California coast between Los Angeles and Santa Barbara the weather was fine. The Pacific Ocean as seen from the front seat of my Cadillac traveling northbound on Highway 101 was azure blue and sparkled with the bright afternoon sun reflecting from wave crests. The further north I traveled the traffic got lighter and lighter until I had the road all to myself as I drove through tiny little beach towns with names like, Mussel Shoals, Carpinteria and Summerland.

§

After I left JoJo's room at the Queen of the Angels Hospital, I drove over to Tommy's and had a chili hamburger for lunch. Next, I pulled into an Esso station on San Pedro Street and had my tank filled with gas. Three attendants swarmed over my Caddie washing my windshield, checking my oil and making sure air pressure in my tires was correct. A few minutes later I saw the attendant remove the hose from my car's filler pipe and reattach it to the gas pump. He walked up to my window and announced that my Cadillac had taken thirteen gallons of Ethyl gas to fill and the bill was $2.34. I paid and drove out of the station and northbound on San Pedro.

When I crossed Sixth Street, in the heart of skid row, I saw a fair sized group of down and outers lined up at the door of a charity kitchen. After pulling my car to the curb near them, I rolled down the passenger window of my car and threw a pair of size 11 Florsheims lace ups out onto the sidewalk. As I drove away, I looked back in the rear view mirror and saw a crowd of bums fighting each other over the shoes.

When I approached Highway 101, I signaled and turned left. Following the highway northwest past Griffith Park and then to Toluca Lake where the 101 turned abruptly west and went on into Ventura County. The trip took me a little over two hours and I arrived in Santa Barbara at about 3:30 in the afternoon. Although it was a city of 45,000 people, Santa Barbara continued to have a sedate small town feel. The main drag was called State Street and that was where most of the bigger businesses were clustered.

§

At the first intersection within the city limits, I saw a beat cop standing on the corner in front of a flower shop and leaning against a blue mail box. I pulled my car to the curb, slid over, cranked down the passenger window and asked the cop for directions to the Saint Gertrude Home for Girls.

The cop's directions were kind of garbled; maybe he'd had one too many "Coca-Colas" at lunchtime, but I eventually found Nopal Street and pulled up in front of Saint Gertrude's. It was in a big red brick building that wasn't maintained very well and was just down the street from Our Lady of Guadalupe Catholic Church. I made my way to the main door and rang that bell.

The door was answered by a young woman in her late twenties wearing a full, black, nun's habit. "Good afternoon. I am Sister Monica, how may I help you?" she asked pleasantly.

"Yes, my name is Matthew Cole. I need to speak to the head nun. It concerns one of your charges," I said.

'Please come in," said Sister Monica. She backed away and escorted me down a dark hallway to an office where I was invited to sit in a chair in front of a desk. "Please be seated. I'll get Sister Martha."

A little while later, Sister Monica was back with another nun. This one was about fifty, who wore glasses and was also in a full habit. She sat down behind the desk and looked at me.

"Hello, I'm Sister Martha. I'm in charge here. How may I help you?" said the nun, with a genuine smile.

"Yes, I'm Matthew Cole and I'm a private investigator. I'm afraid I have some bad news for one of your girls," I said and pushed my P.I. identification card across the desk. The nun picked up the card, looked it over, then laid it back down on the desk.

"Which of my girls?" asked Sister Martha.

"Amelia Carter," I responded. Then, speaking to the nun in short, succinct sentences, I laid out the story of the death of Daisy Carter. I left out most of the lurid details, but I covered all the main points. When I finished I saw the pain in the eyes of the Sister.

"Oh, that poor child, It's never easy to tell a child that she's an orphan." she said.

"I drove all the way up here from Los Angeles to tell you this and also to let you know that I will be taking over the payment for Amelia's room and board," I said.

"Well, that is very generous of you, Mr. Cole. Would you like to meet Amelia?"

"Sure," I answered, even though I wondered if it was a good idea.

Sister Martha looked over at the other nun, who was standing beside the door of the office. "Sister Monica, would you go and get Amelia Carter?" she asked.

While we were waiting, I asked Sister Martha how the girl's home got its funding.

"Oh, the diocese gives us what it can, but we rely on private donations for the indigent girls. A few like Amelia have relatives who pay for their girl's room and board. But every month it seems we think we aren't going to be able to keep the lights on and the gas hooked up for heat. But God is good and He has come through for us so far."

A few minutes later Sister Monica returned. "I'm sorry, Sister Martha, but Amelia wouldn't come unless we brought Lisa with us." The sister was pushing a wheelchair with a somewhat emaciated young girlof about five who had metal braces attached to her legs. Standing beside and holding the hand of the child in the wheelchair was another little girl. She was slim and small with huge brown eyes. She was wearing a little belted blue dress and long dark blue stockings. Her brown hair was parted in the middle and braided into pigtails that hung down her back.

"Amelia, this is Mr. Cole. He wanted to meet you," said Sister Martha to the standing child. The girl just looked at me somberly. I got down on one knee.

"Hi Amelia. I'm Matt," I said

"This is my best friend Lisa. She has polio," answered Amelia, still holding her friend's hand.

"I'm pleased to meet you Lisa. Amelia, how old are you?"

"I'm four-and-a-half."

"Well, it's been a pleasure meeting you, Amelia," I said and stood. I noticed the love and compassion on the two nuns' faces as they looked at the two children. It told me all I needed to know about Saint Gertrude's Home for Girls. It was a happy place filled with love and not a hellhole like some orphanages I had seen.

Sister Monica wheeled Lisa out of the room and Amelia followed, giving me a little wave with her hand as she left.

'Thank you, sister, I want to settle Amelia's bill and maybe make a little contribution before I go," I said, taking my checkbook out of my breast pocket.

"Yes," said Sister Martha, "Amelia's current bill for the last quarter is in the amount of 176 dollars."

I sat back down and wrote a check, then tore it out of the checkbook and handed it to the sister. Sister Martha looked at the check and then abruptly sat down in her chair in shock.

"Mr. Cole, I think you have made a mistake. This check is made out for 52,000 dollars," she said fanning herself with a hand.

"No sister, there's been no mistake. I wish it could have been more but that's all the money I have in the account right now,' I replied.

CHAPTER
TWENTY-TWO

DOWNTOWN
LOS ANGELES
JANUARY 23, 1952
9:30 A.M.

I was driving my Cadillac toward the superior court building on Hill Street downtown. As I drove I reflected on all that had happened in the last month and a half. The day after his son was arraigned for involuntary manslaughter in the death of Daisy Carter, Councilman Michael Conrad Sr. abruptly resigned from the city council. He told reporters for the daily papers that he was quitting politics for good and would henceforth make no further comments on his son's case. The senior Conrad was never charged for his part in covering up the crime. After the case against Conrad Jr. progressed beyond a preliminary hearing and the motions phases, he devastated the local press when his attorney announced that his client would opt for a court trial rather than try the case before a jury. The trial was held in mid-December in department 22 of the superior court in the Hill

Street courthouse, with old Judge Randolph Petersen presiding and lasting barely more than a day. The verdict was "guilty," of the crime of involuntary manslaughter. The reason I was headed to the courthouse was that Judge Petersen was scheduled to pass sentence on Conrad today.

JoJo was out of the hospital and at home with her father recuperating. The last time I talked to her she had said she anticipated returning to work sometime in June. Since November no one had heard a peep from Captain Reed. Every month or so one of the Los Angeles newspapers published a perfunctory article stating that the investigation into the murders of Lt. Brandywine and Sgt. Connors was continuing, but everyone knew that the investigation was as dead as the two crooked cops. After a traditional cop funeral, everyone on the force promptly forgot about Brandywine and Connors. The word around the station houses was that the crooked bastards got in over their heads with the Dragna gang and got what they had coming to them. Also, Chief Parker had kept his word. In late November vice cops raided the Havana Club. Enough documentary evidence related to the call girl ring was uncovered in the office safe to send Duke Gallagher and two of his associates away for 10 years in prison for felony pimping and pandering.

When I arrived at the courthouse on Hill Street, I parked in the south parking lot and hobbled the long block to the main entrance. I took the elevator to the fifth floor and then walked down the hallway to department 22.

When I entered the courtroom I saw that the spectator seating area in front of the bar was only half full. The people sitting in the chairs waiting for the show to start appeared to be members of the press except for two or three elderly "court watchers" sprinkled around in the group. Then, on the right side of the courtroom in the back row, I spotted the huge bulk of Carlo the mountain-and-a-half sitting rigidly and staring straight ahead. He was dressed all in black like he was going to a funeral. I didn't want to bother Carlo so I sat in the back row of seats on the left side.

A little after ten the court bailiff, who was a gray haired L.A. County Sheriff's deputy, got to his feet. "All rise," he said loudly. "In the presence of the flag of our country, emblem of the constitution, and remembering the principles for which it stands, superior court department 22, in and for the County of Los Angeles is now in session, the Honorable Judge Randolph Petersen presiding. Please be seated."

As the audience was sitting down, old Judge Petersen doddered his way from his chambers stage left to the bench and sat down. He was ancient, well over ninety. The talk around the courthouse was that because he had married and divorced eight times in his life, was supporting too many ex-wives t to ever retire. Some of the female staff suggested that he was so creepy that the only way he could get a woman to sleep with him was to marry her. One day the old guy would just keel over on the bench and that would be that. It was rumored that some of the more irreverent courthouse sheriff's deputies had a pool going, betting on the date it would happen.

At this moment Michael Norton Conrad Jr. strode arrogantly into the courtroom from the hallway accompanied by his expensive lawyer and with his father walking behind him. The younger Conrad was dressed in an exquisite gray, double breasted suit. He pushed the swinging door in the bar aside with his knee, strode arrogantly three or four steps and sat down with his attorney at the counsel table on the left. Conrad Sr. sat down in the front row behind his son. The deputy district attorney was already in place at the right table and had been for some time.

'I call the case of the State of California verses Michael Conrad Jr. Let the record reflect that the defendant is present with his counsel and Mr. Morrison is here representing the people. Gentlemen, we're here for sentencing. Mr. Goodwin is your client ready for sentencing?" asked the judge.

"Yes, your honor," answered the big shot lawyer.

"Are the people ready?"

"Yes, your honor," said the deputy D.A. who looked about nineteen years old.

"Let me say first, that I have done a lot of thinking about this case since I found the defendant guilty of involuntary manslaughter a month ago," said the judge, as a preamble. Uh-oh, I thought. I hope you weren't thinking about the case as you counted the stacks of one hundred dollar bills delivered to you by Conrad senior. "I think that this is a case of a young man from a good family who fell in with the wrong crowd. He just went astray for a little while. I think the death of this unfortunate woman was in reality a tragic accident. She has to share some of the blame because of her own choice of occupation," continued Judge Petersen. I couldn't believe the judge was blaming the strangled woman for getting strangled.

"Therefore, since I feel it wouldn't be fair to saddle this young man for life with a felony conviction on his record, I am setting aside my verdict of guilty to involuntary manslaughter and entering a verdict of guilty to solicitation for prostitution, section 647b of the California Penal Code, a misdemeanor. I sentence the defendant to unsupervised probation for a period of two years." The old judge then doddered off the bench. Michael Conrad looked back at his father with a smirk and gave him a thumbs up signal.

I couldn't believe it. I wondered how much the corrupt old codger had gotten out of millionaire Conrad Sr. It was probably enough to give each of his ex-wives a nice bonus on their birthday.

I looked over at Carlo the mountain-and-a-half. He was standing in the last row of seats and staring at Conrad Jr. As I watched, he turned toward the center aisle and our eyes locked for a moment, then the big man quietly walked out of the courtroom. What I had seen in the ex- gangster's eyes wasn't sorrow, resignation, disappointment or even anger as I expected. It was death. Michael Norton Conrad didn't know it but as sure as I was standing there, he was a dead man.

§

It was a Sunday in August 1952. My wife June and I, along with our son Bobby were on the Santa Monica beach enjoying the breeze wafting off the blue water of the Pacific Ocean. I had sunglasses on and was leaning back in a beach chair. Bobby, 16 months old, was busily scooping sand into a plastic bucket with a plastic shovel. When it was full, he would dump out the sand and start over again. I no longer referred to him as Winston because he no longer resembled Churchill. In the last few months my boy had experienced a growth spurt and now he was skinny as a string bean. June was sitting beside us reading the latest issue of Life Magazine.

A very attractive brunette in a skimpy bathing suit sashayed past where we were sitting. Bobby stopped scooping the sand and began to stare up at the babe with his mouth agape in awe. His head turned to follow the woman and he didn't look away until the curvy female had walked out of sight.

"I see the apple didn't fall far from the tree," said June drily, looking at me over the top of her sunglasses.

"That's my boy. If he's doing that already, we'll have to chain him up during full moons by the time he's sixteen, just like Wolf Man," I replied. Laughing, I unfolded a copy of the L.A. Times I had just bought a few minutes ago at a beach kiosk. The front page was full of boring political stuff because there was a national election scheduled for November. On page three though, an article caught my eye.

"Where is Michael Conrad?" queried the caption. Intrigued, I read the article below. It said: "Authorities are baffled by the disappearance of Michael Conrad, 34, a wealthy Los Angeles playboy. On Saturday night at around midnight Conrad left a party in Beverly Hills telling his hosts that he was going straight home. Two hours later a servant at his Laurel Canyon home found his Jaguar sports car parked in the driveway with the driver's door standing open, lights on and the motor running. Conrad was nowhere to be found. Conrad's father, Michael Conrad Sr. is requesting the public's help in locating his son. Anyone with information is requested to call WI 5-2387. A reward is offered."

I would never say anything because of my loyalty to Carlo, but I had a pretty good idea where Michael Conrad Jr. was. I couldn't exactly say for sure, but I had a strong hunch that his lifeless body was at the bottom of a certain thousand foot deep abandoned mineshaft in the Nevada desert that Carlo the mountain-and-a-half and I had reason to remember very well. It's at the head of a meandering canyon about ten miles outside the city limits of Las Vegas.

AUTHOR'S NOTE

Thank you for reading my book. If you enjoyed it, won't you please take a moment to leave me a review at your favorite Retailer? Here is a link to my Author's page on Amazon: https://www.amazon.com/D.W.-Drake/e/B07RDY3M56/ref=ntt_dp_epwbk_0

Thanks!

D. W. Drake

Sign up for email updates and receive free advance reading copies, updates on new releases, special offers and bonus content. You can contact me directly by email: dwdrake@savanatpress.com

You may also sign up at: www.savanatpress.com